'Why do you

David turned round ... said, equally softly, ...

'I'm not the naïve te... you used to know,' she warned.

'I realise that. I like the woman you've become.' And I've never really stopped thinking about you. Wondering what went wrong. Wishing. Most of the time I kept you in the back of my mind, but you were always there. Waiting.

'I really hated you, David. For ruining my life. At the time, I thought the world had ended.'

'I hated you, too. I didn't go out with anyone for three years after you.' They'd hurt each other. Badly. Now perhaps it was time to heal each other. 'Hol…' Words weren't enough. They weren't nearly enough to explain how he felt. What he wanted. What he needed.

Slowly, not quite believing that it was happening, he walked back over to her. Then she was in his arms, and he was kissing her as if he'd been starved of love for the last twelve years.

Dear Reader

I was planning my next book when three doctors leaped into my head and hijacked me! Zoe, Judith and Holly trained together, are best friends and work together at LONDON CITY GENERAL.

Zoe's the clever one, a real high-flyer who's never found love. Until she meets gorgeous Brad, on secondment to Paediatrics from California. Can she heal his broken heart—and can he help her feel less haunted by the secret she hasn't even told her best friends?

Judith's the glamorous one, who delivers babies by day and sings at hospital fundraisers at night. She falls in love with Kieran, the new maternity consultant. But after a discovery threatens to tear their love apart, can she teach him to believe in her—and in himself?

Holly's the 'prickly' one with a soft heart—but it'll take a special man to get close enough to find out! She chose the fast-paced life of the Emergency Department to help her forget her lost love. But when David walks into her life again, will it be second time lucky?

The best bit about working on a trilogy was that I didn't have to say goodbye to my characters. They made appearances in each other's stories! I loved being able to explore a hospital's community and see how different departments work together, and I hope you enjoy life in the fast lane at London City General as much as I did.

With love

Kate Hardy

THE DOCTOR'S PREGNANCY SURPRISE

BY
KATE HARDY

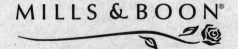

MILLS & BOON®

For Dot—good friend and ace agent—with love

First published in Great Britain 2005
Harlequin Mills & Boon Limited,
Eton House, 18-24 Paradise Road, Richmond, Surrey TW9 1SR

© Pamela Brooks 2005

ISBN 0 263 84294 0

Set in Times Roman 10½ on 12 pt.
03-0305-48021

Printed and bound in Spain
by Litografia Rosés, S.A., Barcelona

CHAPTER ONE

HOLLY blinked hard on her way into the emergency reception area. The man walking down the corridor with Sue, their consultant… No. Of course it wasn't David Neave. Plenty of men had dark hair. She hadn't got a proper look at his face either, just seen the outline of his jaw and nose. So what if they'd reminded her of David? It was highly unlikely that he'd be in the emergency department at London City General.

What was she doing, thinking of him anyway? That part of her life was way behind her. She hadn't thought of him in years.

Well, months.

Well, she *had* had that odd dream last week, the one where he'd been kissing her. It had been so real that she'd actually woken up and turned to cuddle into him. Except, of course, there had been an empty space and an unused pillow beside her. She'd almost been able to taste his mouth on hers, feel the familiar tingle as his fingers skated over her skin.

She shook herself. David Neave might have been the love of her life, but he'd also been the big let-down of her life. A glimpse of a stranger—a man who looked vaguely like him but couldn't possibly be him—shouldn't get to her like this. She'd moved on years ago. Hadn't she?

She saw her next patient—a teenager who'd fallen off a skateboard and had gravel embedded deep in the grazes—and then went to the rest room for some much-needed coffee.

When she opened the door, she stopped dead.

The man she'd seen earlier was there. This time she saw his face rather than his profile, and her heart almost stopped.

It *was* him.

But why here, why now? It had been twelve years since she'd seen him. His dark hair had the odd grey strand in it, there were lines on his face that hadn't been there during sixth form, and his shoulders had broadened, but he still had that charming smile. The one that had almost stopped her heart when he'd come to sit next to her in the sixth form.

That beautiful mouth. The one that had explored every bit of her body. The mouth that had whispered words of love, of passion: promises he'd never kept.

Oh, Lord. One smile and she'd gone right back to being eighteen years old, naïve enough to believe that 'I'll love you till the day I die' really meant that, was more than just the magic words calculated to get him into her knickers.

She reminded herself sharply that she was thirty years old, and a specialist in emergency medicine. Holly the realist, not Holly the dreamer.

God only knew why David Neave was in the middle of the ED rest room at London City General, drinking coffee and chatting to the senior emergency nurse. Unless… A truly nasty thought hit her. Their new senior registrar was due to start today. David, like Holly, had always planned to become a medic. He was in the rest room, not the relatives' room. QED: *he* was their new senior registrar.

Maybe he wouldn't recognise her. She'd changed a lot in the last twelve years, particularly in the first six months. Not that he would have given a damn, because he'd made quite sure he hadn't been around when she'd needed him.

Oh, who was she trying to kid? Despite the years, she

knew exactly who he was. He'd know her, too. Well, she wasn't going to skulk around. London City General was *her* patch. She was going to walk into that room with her head held high and not let him faze her. Everyone knew that Holly Jones was tough. Now was the time to prove it.

'Morning,' she said sweetly, aiming her smile at Anna, the senior sister, rather than their new medic, and slotted money into the chocolate machine.

The machine took her money and bleeped. The little coil of metal twisted round, but the chocolate bar stayed balanced at the end of its row.

Oh, brilliant. Absolutely brilliant. Just when she *needed* the stuff, even more than she needed coffee. A square of chocolate and she could face the world.

Face David Neave.

'Is it playing up again?' Anna asked. 'I'll get Siobhan to call Maintenance.'

'No point. She'll spend all her time batting her eyes at Mitchell and forget to ask him to sort the machine. I'll deal with it.' Holly narrowed her eyes and looked at the machine. 'Now,' she said, her voice quiet but very authoritative. She tapped the glass opposite the chocolate bar she'd paid for. And it fell neatly into the tray at the bottom.

'That's better,' she said, unwrapped the foil and broke off a square. *Yes.* The chocolate rush hit her, and she could cope again.

David wasn't sure which bit he didn't believe. The fact that the vending machine had given her the chocolate on her command—or the fact that he was in the same room as her again. The woman who'd broken his heart when he was eighteen. Holly Jones.

Or maybe this woman was her double.

'Holls, let me introduce you. This is David Neave, our

new senior reg. He started this morning and Sue got called away so she asked me to show him round,' Anna announced. 'David, this is the woman who scares the chocolate machine into submission. Our registrar—'

'Holly Jones,' he cut in. It really *was* her. Except that her dark hair was now cut in a short, functional style instead of being tied back at the nape of her neck, and her grey eyes were much, much harder.

Or maybe they always had been hard but he'd refused to see it.

Anna blinked in surprise. 'You two know each other?'

'We were at school together. A long, long time ago,' Holly said quickly.

Was it his imagination, or was there a twinge of guilt in her eyes? She'd looked away again almost immediately, as if she was too embarrassed to face him. It was a bit late for an attack of conscience now. She should have thought about that twelve years ago.

And now it looked as if he was going to have to work with her.

Holly Jones was back in his life.

Hell. She was even wearing the same perfume. How could such a tiny thing as a spritz of scent take him spinning right back twelve years? The past, when Holly had been in his arms, kissing him and whispering, 'I love you.' Words that had meant everything to him—and absolutely nothing to her.

'We lost touch,' David said.

That was one way of putting it. Because the love of his life had walked out on him when they were eighteen. And her timing had been impeccably bad: she'd done it the week before his A-level exams.

Holly could hardly believe her ears. *Lost touch?* Yeah, right. It had been none of her doing. *He'd* been the one to lose touch. Deliberately. The first sign of trouble, and he'd been out of there. Hadn't returned any of her phone calls, hadn't replied to her letters. When she'd gone to his house to talk it over face to face, he'd been away on holiday. With another girl.

He hadn't accepted responsibility back then, and he certainly wasn't going to admit it now.

What a creep.

More proof—as if she needed it—that she was better off without him.

'So you're from Liverpool, too?' Anna asked.

'I moved away a long time ago,' David said. 'I trained in Southampton.'

Holly knew that. She'd been there the day his offer from Southampton had come through. The same day as hers. They'd been offered places for getting the same grades, even. And they'd planned to go to med school together.

Except she hadn't made it.

And when she'd sat her A levels the following year— and got the straight A grades her teachers had predicted— she'd accepted the offer to train in London. No way could she have faced Southampton, knowing that he was there.

'I worked in Newcastle for a couple of years, then came here,' David said.

She knew he was looking at her. Knew he was expecting her to respond. And Anna expected it, too. If Holly followed her instincts and stomped out of the rest room, Anna would start to wonder. And although the senior sister didn't gossip, the rest of the department did. It wouldn't take long for rumours to fill in the blanks. The worst thing was, the wildest ones would probably be right on target. 'I trained here,' she said shortly.

Then she met his eyes, and wished she hadn't. Because,

for an instant, she'd seen a flash of yearning there. A yearning that was immediately echoed in her own heart.

She slammed the brakes on. There was no going back now. Working with David was going to be awkward, but she didn't have a choice. Not unless she wanted them both to be the centre of gossip for an uncomfortably long time.

'You two must have a lot to catch up on,' Anna said.

Over my dead body! Holly thought. She couldn't help looking at David, and was surprised to see questions in his eyes. Did he expect her to fill him in on her gap year—what had really happened? He hadn't cared enough to find out at the time. Why did he want to know now, when it was much too late?

'Years,' David said, in answer to Anna's question.

Though it underlined Holly's thoughts. It was *years* too late for them.

'It won't take you long to settle in, then, seeing as you know each other. Sue put you on the same team,' Anna said.

The blood rushed straight from Holly's head and it was an effort to keep upright, her head was spinning so much. David was going to be working on *her* team? Given the new shift rotations they were doing, it meant she'd be spending every single moment at work near him. Forty-odd hours a week.

She tried to school her face into neutral and stared at his hands, hoping that she could think of some suitable response quickly enough to stop Anna asking questions. But looking at his hands was a bad, bad move—because she could still remember the pressure of his fingertips against her skin. Still remember what those hands had done to her. Why couldn't she get him out of her head?

'Holls? Are you all right?' Anna asked.

'Uh—yes. I hit traffic problems so I didn't get back from

Liverpool until pretty late last night. I, um, just need some sleep,' Holly prevaricated. It was true, up to a point. What she really wanted was time to think, not time to sleep. She gave a huge yawn and hoped it didn't look as fake as it felt.

Give me time. Give me space to deal with this, she begged. And, right on cue, her pager bleeped. She checked it. 'Sorry. Gotta dash. Catch you later, Anna, David.' She gave them both her best smile and left the rest room with indecent haste.

'Fancy you two knowing each other. Still, at least we don't have to warn you that Holls isn't as scary as she seems,' Anna said.

David frowned. Holly—*his* Holly—scary? Surely they couldn't be talking about the same person. Holly had been the epitome of 'sweet sixteen'. She'd been lovely. A little shy, but once David had got to know her he'd discovered her sense of fun.

Holly Jones, *scary*?

'She tells it like it is, and God help you if you make a stupid mistake,' Anna said, rolling her eyes. 'But if anyone needs help, she's the first one to offer.' She smiled. 'But I expect you already know all this.'

'Yes,' David lied. Maybe he'd been so in love with her that it had blinded him to her real self. If anyone had told him that Holly would dump him without an explanation, he'd have scoffed. He and Holly had told each other everything, even the secret dreams nobody else had known about.

Obviously he'd never really known her. Because the Holly Jones he remembered had planned to be a GP—so she could get to know her patients properly and look after them from cradle to grave. He'd felt the same. They'd even talked about having their own practice, a husband-and-wife team.

Even though he'd chosen his speciality years after their break-up, he hadn't been able to face a GP rotation. Instead, he'd chosen emergency medicine, where he could do the best for his patients but he could stay uninvolved. He could walk away.

'Right, now you've finished your coffee, I'll show you round the rest of the department,' Anna said.

'Thanks.' He smiled at Anna. So what if Holly was back in his life? She was probably married—to someone her family thought suitable for her—and used her maiden name for professional purposes. And even if she wasn't married, David was older and much, much wiser. He wasn't going to let her get close ever again.

As for her smile making his heart turn over, that was just a reflex action. He hadn't thought of Holly for ages.

Ha. Who was he trying to kid? At the weekend, when he'd moved into his tiny flat round the corner from the hospital, he'd unpacked a few boxes and come across an old photograph of the two of them together. A photograph he should have thrown out years and years ago. He'd looked at her sweet, shy smile and wondered what she was doing now. Had she become a doctor? Was she married to another GP, with four children and a houseful of cats and dogs and hamsters, living the life they'd always planned, only without him?

Now he knew at least one of the answers. She was a doctor. An emergency specialist. They were going to have to work together and put the past behind them. Somehow.

'It's my stomach, doctor,' Lucy said, doubling over as another spasm hit her. 'It hurts so much.'

'Lie back, try to relax and I'll take a look,' Holly said gently. 'Breathe for me. In, out, in, out.'

Gradually Lucy calmed and lay back against the bed.

Holly bared Lucy's abdomen and palpated it gently. 'Tell me when it hurts,' she said.

Lucy flinched wherever Holly touched her. 'It hurts all over.'

An acute abdomen could mean one of about a dozen things. Holly had to narrow things down. Fast. 'Have you had any other symptoms?'

Lucy grimaced. 'I thought it was just a bug—the usual thing, a temperature and a headache and feeling a bit sweaty and tired. I've had that horrible summer cough and that makes everyone a bit breathless, doesn't it?'

'Maybe,' Holly said.

'It's so hot in here,' Lucy said, then shook her head. 'Sorry. I'm trying not to whine.'

'You're not feeling well,' said Holly. 'And we all think we need air-conditioning, too.'

'I was going to see my GP. I was starting to think maybe it was the menopause, even though I'm not quite forty.'

'Because of the sweats?'

'And my periods are next to nothing,' Lucy said. She smiled wryly. 'And I've been getting PMT. I mean, really *bad* PMT. Oliver'll tell you, I've been a monster.' Her hand tightened round his. 'But then I got this pain in my stomach.'

'I thought it might be her appendix so I brought her here,' said Oliver, Lucy's husband.

'Have you been sick at all?' Holly asked.

Lucy nodded. 'And I've had a bit of a tummy upset. It might have been something I ate.'

'She's been eating like a horse lately,' Oliver said.

'I don't think it's appendicitis,' Holly said. She checked

Lucy's temperature and pulse. Lucy's pulse was definitely up—more than Holly had expected from the fever. 'Have you had any other pains lately?'

'She won't admit it, but she's had chest pains,' Oliver said.

'I am *not* having a heart attack. Will you stop nagging me, Oliver?' Lucy said crossly. 'Besides, I'm managing my weight so my heart'll be fine. I'm on that new diet and it's actually working.' Despite the fact that, according to Oliver, Lucy had been eating a lot more than usual.

'Have you lost much weight?' Holly asked.

'A stone and a half. It's falling off,' Lucy said. 'First time ever.'

'Probably because you never stop. She's always on the go,' Oliver added wryly. 'She's just been promoted to head teacher.'

'So I need to put the hours in,' Lucy said defensively.

'I need to do some blood tests to rule out some possibilities,' Holly said. 'I'll be back in a second.' She smiled and left the cubicle.

'Miche—just the woman I wanted,' she said, spotting the staff nurse. 'Can you give me a hand running some tests, please?'

'Sure. What do you need?'

'My patient's in cubicle eight. Her name's Lucy. I need some bloods done, first. Us and Es, ionised calcium, full blood count and differential. Ask the lab to check T4, T3 and TSH as well.' Checking the tri-iodothyronine, thryoxine and thyroid stimulating hormone levels in the bloodstream would help Holly find out if it was a problem with Lucy's endocrine system, and if so the results would help her give the right dosage of medication to get Lucy's levels back to normal.

'What's this? A patient with thyroid problems?' a male voice asked beside her.

Damn. She could do with some kind of early warning system so she could avoid David—so she could avoid situations like this when he might catch her off guard. 'I'm not sure. That's why I'm asking for T4, T3 and TSH levels,' she said shortly, and turned her attention back to Michelle. 'Thanks, Miche. I'd also like to do some BMGs.' BMGs, or bedside strip measurement of glucose, would check Lucy's blood-sugar levels. 'And a mid-stream urine specimen— Oh, and she's got a bit of a chest infection, so ask the lab to run blood cultures, so we can see what's causing it.'

'What are her symptoms?' David asked.

'Acute abdomen, losing weight despite eating a lot, chest pains, a fast heartbeat, sweating, volatile emotions and tiredness.'

'What about her blink rate?' If Lucy was blinking less than normal, it was another pointer towards a thyroid problem. 'Any swelling in the tissues around her eyes?'

Holly looked at him and had to fight to get her thoughts back in control. Hell, this was just how she'd imagined him as a doctor. Completely focused on his patients. Caring.

If only he'd been like that about *her*. 'I'm doing bloods to check if it's thyroid,' Holly said.

'I nearly specialised in endocrinology before I settled on emergency medicine. I could have word with her, if you like.'

No. I don't want to work with you and I don't want you interfering with my patients.

On the other hand, she'd taken the Hippocratic oath. She had a choice of letting David help or trying to get hold of Fabian, the endocrine specialist, who almost never answered his bleep and needed at least three follow-up nags.

Her patient came first. Even if it meant that Holly was in the awkward position of owing David Neave a favour. 'Thanks. I'll introduce you.'

To her relief, he simply followed her back to cubicle eight. 'Lucy, Oliver, this is David Neave, our new senior registrar. I've been talking to him about what the problem might be, and he's your man for any questions.'

He used to be *my* man.

She pushed the thought away. The past was over. *Over.*

She forced a smile to her face. 'Michelle, our staff nurse, is going to come and take blood for tests.' She didn't quite trust her hands to be as steady as usual if she had to take the blood under David's gaze, and Lucy really didn't need half a dozen puncture wounds from an incompetent doctor.

'Do you mind if I have a look at your hand?' David asked. He pinched the skin on the back of Lucy's hand, very gently, as Holly watched. When the skin didn't flatten again instantly, Holly knew that Lucy was dehydrated.

'Has anyone in your family had problems with their thyroid gland?' he asked.

'Not that I can think of. Why?' Lucy asked.

'Holly told me about your symptoms and I think your thyroid gland's overactive. What you're suffering from is something called thyroid storm.'

'Is it serious?' Oliver asked.

Yes. If it went untreated, one in ten cases would die.

'We can do something about it,' David reassured them both. 'Holly's arranged the blood tests, we'll give you some paracetamol to get your temperature down, a saline drip to help with the dehydration, some antithyroid medication to deal with the excess thyroid hormones and some beta-blockers to help slow your heart rate down to what it should be.'

'Heart medicine? But…' Lucy shook her head. 'What's wrong with my heart?'

'It's all to do with your thyroid gland producing too many hormones. The thyroid gland is just here in your throat, underneath your voice-box,' David explained.

When he touched Holly's throat, to demonstrate, her pulse went into overdrive and she only hoped that he couldn't feel the frantic flutter.

'It produces the hormones that regulate your body's energy levels and at the moment it's producing too much.'

'That's why you're eating so much,' Holly said, hoping her voice sounded less shaky than it felt. 'Your body's metabolism is working too hard, making you feel hungry so you want to eat, but you're still losing weight.'

'It's also making your heart beat faster than it should,' David added.

So's mine, Holly thought in desperation. And it shouldn't be. I don't want it to.

'Thyroid problems? Isn't that something old people get?' Lucy asked.

'No. It's more common in women, and usually it's young to middle-aged women, in their thirties to fifties,' Holly said.

'If you've got an overactive thyroid but you haven't been treated for it, and then you get an infection or you're under a lot of stress, you can end up with thyroid storm. We'll need to get you admitted because we'll need to run more tests,' David said. When Lucy coughed, he said, 'We also want to know what's causing your cough, so we can treat that, too.' He looked at Holly. 'Can you ask a porter to bring a fan in to make Lucy more comfortable, please?'

'You don't have to do that if it's going to mean someone else will be all hot and sticky,' Lucy said.

'It won't,' Holly said. If necessary, she'd use the fan

from her own office—she could manage without for a couple of hours. 'We want your temperature down.'

'Cool air, tepid sponging and paracetamol should do it,' David explained with a smile.

Lucy groaned. 'That's what you do to babies! I feel such an idiot. I should have gone to see my GP when it all started, but I was busy and I didn't want to waste his time.'

'It might have saved you ending up in here,' Holly agreed wryly. 'But if it makes you feel any better, I would've done exactly the same.'

Yes, David thought bitterly, watching her retreating back. Holly had always done things her way, and to hell with the consequences. Even though he had the nasty suspicion that it was going to rake open old wounds, he knew they had to talk.

An hour and a half later—by which time Holly had calmed down a hysterical toddler and removed a bead from his nose, put a dislocated elbow back in place and removed broken glass from a nasty wound and then stitched it—she was in definite need of caffeine.

'I'm taking five,' she told Michelle, and headed for the rest room.

She'd just fixed herself a black coffee from the vending machine, poured the top quarter off and added enough cold water so she could drink it straight down, when David walked in.

'Strong stuff, is it?' he asked, seeing her holding the coffee-cup beneath the tap on the water cooler.

'No. Just temperature regulation,' she said, and drank her coffee. 'Ah. I needed that.' A caffeine fix might just jolt her body back into reality and stop it overreacting any time he came anywhere near her.

'Holly,' he said quietly.

Unwillingly, she faced him. Looked him in the eye. Was that regret she saw there? 'What?'

'I had no idea you worked here.'

She shrugged. 'Why should you?'

He sighed. 'I think we need to talk.'

Way too dangerous. On the ward, she could cope; in a quiet corner in a bar, it would be too much like old times. Just the two of them. 'There's nothing to say.'

'We need to clear the air.'

'There's nothing to say,' she repeated. Nothing either of them could say would change what had happened.

He raked a hand through his hair and she watched his fingers, mesmerised. She could still remember them running through her own hair. Hair that she'd had cut short the moment she'd recognised the truth, to wipe out the memories. Except it hadn't really worked.

'What happened between us was a long time ago.'

Was this his idea of an apology? It certainly wasn't hers!

'And in the emergency department we need to be able to work as a team.'

He'd phrased that very carefully. Good. Because if he'd dared to say anything about being able to rely on each other, she would have murdered him. 'Of course,' she said, as neutrally as she could.

'We're going to have to work together. And it's better if we can do it without…problems.'

Did he think that she was going to weep and wail and ask him why he'd done it? No. Been there, done that, worn the T-shirt—when she was eighteen. She was older. Much wiser. So she could feel relieved that she'd had a very, very lucky escape. And she most certainly wasn't going to act on that flicker of attraction. Blue eyes spelled danger. She didn't make the same mistakes twice. 'Of course,' she said again.

At least he hadn't suggested that they could be friends. Because she didn't think she could go that far. Just in case he was entertaining the idea, she leapt in fast to state the ground rules. 'We're perfectly capable of being colleagues.'

'Good.'

Just to underline the point, she added, 'How's Lucy?'

'Fine. I've just had the results back and they're pretty much what I expected, so I've written up the drugs and admitted her. How come she didn't go to her GP before? She must have had symptoms.'

'She's just been promoted. She's been busy at work, thought maybe she was going through the menopause early and she'd picked up a bug that was doing the rounds.'

'A pulmonary bug?'

Holly nodded, knowing that a pulmonary infection was the most common event that could spark off a thyroid storm. 'Thanks for seeing her for me.'

'Pleasure.'

She wished he hadn't said that word. She scrunched her cardboard cup into a ball and threw it at the bin. It went straight in first time. 'I'd better get back to my patients. I told Michelle I was just taking five minutes. And we're short today.'

'Right.'

She'd half expected him to say, See you. But he hadn't. Just as well. Because she didn't want to see David any more than she had to.

Did she?

CHAPTER TWO

IT WASN'T working.

Holly gritted her teeth, adjusted the incline on the treadmill and increased the speed. But running uphill to the beat of the rock music she was playing on headphones—even at high volume—wasn't enough to drown out her thoughts. It wasn't enough to stop her remembering.

The past is *over*, she reminded herself harshly. You got through it. You don't have to go back there. You're thirty years old, you're a registrar in the emergency department and everybody at London City General respects you. You are *not* eighteen years old with your world collapsing round your ears. Get a *grip*.

But the pep-talk didn't work.

Even though she knew it was pointless and stupid and wasn't going to change anything—yada, yada, yada—she still couldn't get David out of her head. Couldn't stop the memories replaying. David, leaning over her in the orchard next to her parents' house. Those blue, blue eyes, the same colour as a midsummer sky, glittering with love and laughter. The smile on his face, making him more handsome than ever—and then suddenly growing serious as he lowered his mouth to hers. Kissed her. Made love with her, their textbooks and revision forgotten. Skin to skin with sunlight dappling over them, the scent of apple blossom in the air and the sound of birdsong all around.

Stop. Just *stop*. Holly slammed the 'stop' button on the treadmill, switched off the music and leaned with her arms on the supports and her forehead resting on her arms.

She hadn't thought about this for years. Hadn't allowed herself to think about it for years.

Oh, who was she trying to kid? She faced it every time there was an obstetric emergency. Every time a child was brought in. Faced it for a second, blanked it and made the professional in her take over. She was a doctor. First, last and always. Nothing else.

And yet her hands crept instinctively to her flat stomach. Rubbed. Splayed in the protective gesture that all newly pregnant women made, cradling the little life in their womb.

The little life hadn't been there for long. Just long enough to disappoint her parents—nice, middle-class Mr and Mrs Jones, in their big house in the posh bit of Liverpool, with their orchard and their two big cars and their terribly nice, clever children.

Ha. She'd hit eighteen and she'd let them down. Her brother Daniel had waited until he was nineteen before he'd gone off the rails, and he still wasn't quite back on them. They'd both been a disappointment. And Holly's career hadn't quite redeemed her in her parents' eyes. After all, she was in east London, practically the slums as far as they were concerned, when she could have lived somewhere so much more upmarket.

'Holly, how could you be so stupid?'

The words echoed again and again in her head, in her mother's cut-glass tones.

Stupid. She'd been that all right. Stupid enough to think that David would stand by her. OK, so it would have changed their plans a bit, having a baby. A lot, even. She'd have had to take a gap year for starters. But there were nurseries, day-care centres, crèches. They could have coped. Studied together and watched their baby grow up into a toddler and start primary school. Qualified. Moved to a little cottage in the country where they'd have been the village GPs, with four children, a couple of dogs and a rabbit and a guinea pig and maybe a pony for the kids.

Everything they'd wanted. Just as they'd planned—except one of the children would have been a teensy bit older.

Holly took a shuddering breath, willing herself not to cry. She'd cried enough over David the day she'd phoned him to tell him the news. The news that she'd gone into Liverpool the previous day and bought a pregnancy testing kit from a chemist's where nobody had known her or would report back to her mother. She'd done the test secretly that morning. Squirreled the test stick back to her bedroom and watched for five agonisingly slow minutes until the results had shown up. And then she'd known her missed periods and nausea had been nothing to do with exam stress.

Except he hadn't been there.

And he hadn't returned her call—that day, or the next, when she'd phoned him again. She'd believed in David. He wouldn't let her down. He wouldn't desert her when she needed him most...

But he hadn't called her back. It had reached the point where Holly had suspected he'd actually told his mum to lie on the phone and tell Holly that he wasn't there.

He'd been doing biology A level, so he'd have been perfectly capable of working it out for himself. Missed periods probably equalled baby. But he had also been a teenage boy. Full of testosterone and panic. It had taken her long enough to work it out, but in the end she had appreciated his logic. Warped, but understandable. He'd gone for the easy way out. If he didn't contact her again, his girlfriend would eventually realise that he'd dumped her. No mess, nothing to face, nice and clean.

For him.

Not for her.

At least her parents hadn't gloated. Hadn't gone into the I-told-you-so routine. Laura Jones had simply held her daughter and gone into organisation mode. Not for nothing was Laura the chair of the local WI, the Rotary Group and the local school governors.

'We'll get through this. You know you can't possibly keep the baby. Not unless you want to ruin your career before you've even started. So I'll get you booked in somewhere to deal with it. Concentrate on your exams—and we'll get your exam centre changed. You can sit them without having to worry about seeing him.'

Holly hadn't wanted a termination. OK, so the baby hadn't been planned, and the father didn't want to know, but plenty of people coped in the same situation. Maybe once the baby was born, her mother would come round to her way of thinking. She'd get decent A-level grades, take a gap year, then start her course when her baby was around nine months old.

If her parents wouldn't support her, she'd find a way. She'd become a damned good doctor, and she'd be all the family her baby would ever need. She'd do it all on her own if she had to.

Except it hadn't turned out like that.

It had all come crashing down, two hours before her first A-level exam.

Holly scrubbed at her eyes. Stop being such a wimp, she told herself fiercely. You've got everything you want in London. The best possible friends and the best possible job—a job where every single minute's different. And where there wasn't any time to think and wonder about what might have been.

So what if her two best friends had both just got married and she'd been their bridesmaids? So what if, a year or two down the line, Zoe and Jude would have babies and ask Holly to be godmother?

It didn't change her plans. Not at all.

And neither did David's arrival. He was her colleague and they were going to be working the same shifts, but she didn't need to have that much contact with him. They'd agreed to be polite to each other and work as a team, for the sake of the ward. That was enough.

Outside London City General, she'd stay well clear of him. She wasn't going to get sucked back into that old attraction. She wasn't going to fall for those beautiful blue eyes. Or the well-shaped mouth that knew exactly where and how she liked being kissed. Or the clever hands that she'd known would be gentle with patients but were passionate with her.

Get a grip, Holls, she told herself again. Physically, he's your type. And, yes, the sex was good. But that was in another life, another world. It was over between you *years* ago. He's probably married. Married, with children. She linked her hands across her abdomen and pulled tight to take away the emptiness, the memories of the child they'd made who hadn't been born. And even if he isn't, he's not the kind you can rely on. He's not worth it. Just forget him.

So who was the real Holly Jones?

The question had been nagging at David all day. And even an hour's unbroken swim hadn't driven the question out of his head.

Who was she?

She was a doctor. Caring. Kind to patients—he'd discovered that she'd lent her own fan to Lucy, their patient with the thyroid storm, before Lucy had been transferred to the ward. It was the kind of thing that the Holly he remembered would have done.

But she had a reputation here for being that little bit unapproachable. Scary. And she'd been ambitious enough to dump him just before their A levels, concentrating on her work rather than her relationship. She'd even made arrangements to sit her exams elsewhere—and when she hadn't turned up at Southampton he'd realised the truth. She never had wanted to do the village GP thing with him. She'd just been playing with him, marking time. Holly Jones had gone off to conquer the world.

His mum had been the one to tell him.

'Sorry, son. She rang while you were out. She doesn't want to see you any more.'

He hadn't believed her. His mother had never liked Holly, saying that she was stuck-up and was only slumming it with David to pass the time. He'd always been able to shrug it off, until he'd gone down to the phone box on the corner to ring Holly. And then he'd spoken to her mum.

'Sorry, David. She doesn't want to see you again.'

'I'd just like to speak to her, please, Mrs Jones.'

'I'm afraid she won't come to the phone. She really doesn't want to be bothered with you, David.'

He'd refused to leave it at that. As soon as he talked to Holly they'd be able to sort out the problem, whatever it was. He *knew* it. So he'd tried hanging about in the street in the hope that he would see her. But the one occasion when he'd seen her get into her mother's car she'd averted her eyes. She'd refused even to *look* at him.

Then David had finally realised that his mother was telling the truth after all. Holly had grown bored with him. She hadn't even had the guts to tell him to his face that it was over. So maybe his mother's prejudices had been right all along.

He grimaced and went for a shower. The water was almost scalding hot but he didn't feel it. Didn't feel anything.

Because Holly was back in his life.

Holly. The woman who'd ruined him for relationships. The woman who'd been a ghost throughout his marriage—as his ex-wife had thrown at him the day she'd walked out on him.

He'd learned not to do relationships any more. So now he was a dedicated doctor. A good one. He'd be able to treat Holly as just another colleague.

Wouldn't he?

The emergency department was trialling a different way of working shifts: instead of the usual internal rotation of two or three earlies plus two or three lates for three weeks, then four nights in the fourth week, they were trying two earlies, two lates, two nights, four off. Which would have been fine by David if Holly hadn't been on his team—because her shifts were identical to his.

If he asked for a change, people would notice. Especially as he'd admitted to knowing her at school. The hospital grapevine was definitely stronger here than it had been in Southampton or Newcastle, and he didn't want to become the focus of gossip. He knew Holly wouldn't take it well either. So he had to put up and shut up.

His doubts lessened as the week went on because Holly stuck to the rules: she treated him as just another colleague, giving him as much information as he needed about patients and steering well clear of anything remotely personal. Which suited him fine.

Until the Friday night, when David was treating a patient with chest pains and heard an almighty racket coming from Reception.

He glanced at the clock. Yep, just as he'd thought: chucking-out time from the pubs. It sounded as if there were a number of drunken people wandering round

Reception, demanding treatment. Probably a punch-up, he thought. Bruises, lacerations, the odd fracture.

But they'd probably demand immediate treatment and would harry the receptionist until they were seen. Which meant he needed to step in before things escalated.

'I'll be back in a moment,' he promised the elderly man. 'Keep breathing the oxygen for me. Slow breaths. In and one and out and one,' he counted, checking that his patient was keeping the same time. 'That's great. If the pain gets any worse, press the buzzer here.'

Oh, great. Just what they didn't need on a busy Friday night. Six men in their early twenties who'd all drunk way too much beer. Probably with a few vodka or tequila chasers. And they were getting aggressive with Siobhan.

If she didn't do something, right now, this could escalate into something really nasty.

Holly strode over to them. 'I believe you gentlemen require assistance?'

As she'd hoped, they turned away from Siobhan, giving the receptionist a chance to hit the panic button. All Holly needed to do now was to keep them talking until Security arrived.

'You going to kiss it better for me, then?' One of them swaggered over to her.

I'll kick it, more like, if you don't put a sock in it, Holly thought, but she smiled sweetly. She'd had it drummed into her at medical school that you treated all patients the same, even if you didn't like them. Conflict slowed things down and made it more likely that you'd make a clinical error. You had to defuse volatile situations as quickly as you could.

'I know you need to be seen, but Friday nights are always really busy, and, I'm sorry, that means you're in a queue. We'll be able to treat you much more quickly if you wait in a line and give our receptionist the details she needs—one at a time. If you're all talking at once she's not going to be able to hear you properly and that's how mistakes get made.'

'Bossy. Bet you like it on top, don'tcha?' The one with the black eye leered at her. 'You can give me one, if you like.'

She laughed it off. 'I can tell *you've* had a bump on the head.'

'Oi, you've got to see our mate. Now. He's been knifed—he's bleeding,' one of them said, jabbing a finger in the air at her.

Holly kept her arms calmly by her sides and flexed her fingers to avoid her gut reaction of balling her fists ready to punch him. 'We'll see you all in time. But there's one thing you should all know.'

'Yeah?'

She beckoned the one with the black eye closer. 'If you're drunk, I'll have to assume your body won't be able to tolerate any anaesthetic—because it'll make you ill,' she said quietly. This wasn't strictly true, but she was banking on his knowledge of medicine being confined to TV dramas. 'With a bloke your size, I'm going to have to use a *big* needle to stitch your wounds. Without anaesthetic, it's going to hurt.'

'Needle?' Black-Eye said, colour draining from his face.

Just as she'd calculated: the bigger the braggart, the more fuss he made about things hurting. Particularly needles. '*Big* needle,' she emphasised. 'And, of course, I'll need to give you a tetanus booster.' From years of experience, she kept an empty epidural syringe in her pocket when she did the night shift on Fridays or Saturdays, for just this sort of situation. She withdrew it and showed it to him.

He swore in horror. 'That—that's *huge*!'

Which was the whole point: even without the needle, it looked impressive. Her patient didn't need to know the syringe was used for anaesthesia and guiding a tube into the spinal cord—it certainly wasn't used to give vaccinations or local anaesthetic for suturing wounds! She managed to hide her grin. 'If you sit quietly and don't hassle the other patients—or my receptionist—I'll assume you're not drunk and I'll make sure you get some painkillers before I sort out that cut. So it's your choice, mate. Drunk and painful, or not drunk and painkillers?'

'Right.' Black-Eye looked thoughtful. 'Come on, lads. Let's do what the doc says. Sit down and wait.'

'I'm not waiting. That bastard sliced my arm. I'll bleed to death! I want it stitched *now*, so I can go and sort him out,' another one said, thrusting his face belligerently into Holly's. 'You a doc or a dolly?'

She nearly gagged at the alcohol fumes. 'A doctor. A female doctor. One who's been on her feet all evening and really, really needs a cup of coffee. The longer you keep me here, the longer it'll take to treat you. So why don't you sit down and let me finish helping my patient, so I can start seeing to your arm?'

He glared back at her, but he sat down, just as two burly security men entered the room and David emerged from the cubicles.

'Problems?' one of the security men asked.

'Not any more—are there, lads?' Holly asked.

'No, Doc,' Black-Eye said politely.

David stared at Holly. 'What did you do?' he asked.

'Not a lot. Just pointed out a few things.' She shrugged. 'Siobhan, who's next on my list?'

Holly had just taken on six drunken men—all of whom were a good six inches taller than she was. All muscular, all drunk, and all of them had been fighting, so adrenaline was pumping through their bodies, and they'd been raising hell in Reception.

Without even raising her voice, she'd got them all to sit down. Without a fuss. Then had coolly asked to see her next patient.

The sweet, gentle Holly Jones he'd known definitely wouldn't have been able to do that. She'd lived a sheltered life and had probably never even seen anyone drunk or violent—whereas he'd lived on a rough estate where he'd seen situations like this every single night.

So maybe the real Holly *was* the scary one.

Maybe Holly had turned into her mother, the most formidable woman David had ever met.

'Our Holls is pretty amazing, isn't she?' Siobhan said wryly.

'Just remind me never to get on her bad side,' David replied.

Though he didn't think she could do anything else to him. She'd already put him through the mangle and hung him out to dry.

When David had finished treating his share of the drunken brawlers, he headed for the rest room. He needed coffee. Now.

Holly was already there, curled up with a cup of coffee and a chocolate brownie.

Food. He needed *food*. 'Where did you get that?' he asked, eyeing the brownie. He just hoped the shop was still open, wherever it was. And still had something like that left.

He was disappointed. 'Zoe from Paeds left it for me. I'm one of her testers for new recipes.'

'Oh.'

He *wasn't* going to ask her for a bite. Even though he was starving.

But it must have shown on her face because she rolled her eyes. 'All right, all right, I'll split it with you.' She broke the cake in two and handed one half to him, with just the hint of a smile.

'Thank you.' His head was reeling. This was Scary Holly, the one who'd made the drunken louts behave like lambs. How could she be Nice Holly, who shared her goodies? Especially, he thought when he took his first bite, something as scrummy as this, which any normal person definitely wouldn't have wanted to share?

'Enjoyed your first week here?' she asked.

'Yes.' Once he'd got over the shock of seeing her again. But she was being friendly enough to him. He could handle this, treat her as a colleague. Ignore the tingle at the base of his spine every time he looked at her mouth. 'This shift pattern takes some getting used to, though.'

'Give it six months, then the human resources bods will come up with another clever idea for us to try.'

'Such cynicism in one so young,' he teased.

He'd obviously hit a raw nerve, because her face changed. Became shuttered and cool.

What had he said?

He backtracked, fast. 'I was impressed with the way you handled that lot out there.'

She shrugged. 'You get used to it. Most Friday and Saturday nights we get the same sort of thing. It's just a matter of defusing the situation before things get out of hand. Give them a choice so they don't feel they're going to lose face, and they'll usually shut up.'

'They could have hit you.'

'Security were on their way.'

'You still took a risk.' A stupid risk, and it made him want to protect her—despite the fact she'd already proved she was tough, not the sweet and gentle middle-class girl he'd known years ago. She didn't even have that posh accent any more.

'There's a little trick that a registrar taught me when I was still a house officer.' She withdrew the epidural syringe from her pocket. 'You're drunk and you're hurt and the doctor tells you this is what she's going to have to use for your tetanus booster, because when you're drunk you need more medication—though if you wait your turn without a fuss she'll assume you're sober and use a smaller syringe. Are you going to hit her or are you going to shut up and sit down?'

'That's an epidural kit, without the needle.' David stared at her. 'And it's not true about vaccinations. You *didn't*.'

'It was a white lie.' She grinned. 'And it worked, didn't it?' She finished her coffee. 'I'd better get back and see how we're doing out there.'

David gulped his coffee as he watched her leave the room. That smile. It would be so, so easy to forget what had happened between them. To fall for Holly again. She was brave and funny—and beautiful. She'd been pretty as a teenager, but she'd lost that plump ripeness. Thinner, older, with that gamin haircut showing off her incredible bone structure, Holly Jones was beautiful.

But he wasn't going to let her break his heart a second time.

CHAPTER THREE

SATURDAY night was even busier than Friday had been, so Holly barely had a chance to talk to David during the shift. Just when she was going to take a break, Rick, one of the paramedics, brought in a young man.

'His name's Gary—I couldn't get a second name out of his mates. Collapsed in the middle of a nightclub. His mates say it's drink.'

'But you don't think so?'

'Nope.' Rick ran through the usual handover, noting Gary's pulse, breathing rate and his GCS, or Glasgow coma scale, level, which told Holly how the patient was reacting to stimulation. 'He's been drifting in and out of consciousness on the way here. His mates are waiting outside. Want me to send one of them in to see if you can prise anything out of them?'

'Please.' Holly smiled at him. 'Thanks, Rick.'

'Any time, sugar.'

She turned to her patient. 'Hello, Gary. My name's Holly. Do you know where you are?'

The young man looked confused. 'Dunno. Head hurts.'

'You're in London City General. I'm just going to check you over, OK?'

His pulse was way too fast. She shone a torch into his eyes and discovered that his pupils were dilated. He was sweating and a quick examination showed her that he had increased muscle tone. So he must have taken amphetamines of some sort. 'Gary? What did you take tonight?'

'Nothing.' Gary leaned over the side of the bed and was promptly sick.

Before Holly could reach for a kidney dish to catch the vomit, a hand had already pushed one under Gary's chin. 'Here you go, mate.'

She winked at Rick. 'Just in time. Thanks.'

'Pleasure. I've brought Gary's friend in to have a word with you.'

'I'm Holly Jones, the registrar,' she said. The young man looked so nervous that she didn't ask him his name in case it made him bolt. It was more important to find out more about her patient. 'Can you tell me a bit more about Gary?'

'He just collapsed.'

Holly nodded. 'Has he taken anything?'

'No. Just drink.'

She raised an eyebrow. 'Look, I'm not here to lecture you. I'm not going to grass you up to the police or anything like that. I just need to know what he's taken so I can treat him properly.' She spread her hands. 'I've seen enough drunks in my time here to know when someone's drunk. Gary doesn't smell of booze. What did he take?'

'He hasn't taken *nothing*.'

'It looks like amphetamines to me. Ecstasy?'

The young man looked at her for a moment, then sighed, as if knowing that he was beaten. 'No. He couldn't get no disco biscuits. He bought some Eve.'

Eve, or MDEA, was a type of amphetamine similar to Ecstasy. 'Thanks,' Holly said. 'Do you have any idea how long ago he took it?'

'Forty minutes—something like that, I guess.'

'Great.' She smiled reassuringly at him. 'Now I know just what to give your mate to get his body back to normal.'

'He is going to be OK, isn't he?'

'It's too early to say, I'm afraid—though you did the

right thing by calling the ambulance. If you want to wait in the relatives' room, I can come and see you later to let you know how he's getting on.'

'Right.' The young man bit his lip. 'He's been doing it for a while. E, I mean. And Eve. I thought he knew what he was doing. But this bloke offered him some cheap. I never saw him before. Must have been dodgy.'

'It happens.' And the friends and family were left to pick up the pieces. Holly knew that only too well—both as a doctor and as a relative.

'You're really not going to have a go about how drugs are bad for you?'

She shrugged. 'Not my place. And you're old enough to know that for yourself.'

'Yeah.' He smiled wryly back at her.

'There's a coffee-machine in the corridor outside the relatives' room, if you need it. There's a vending machine for chocolate, too.'

'Cheers.'

Holly turned back to her patient. Since he'd taken the drugs less than an hour ago, activated charcoal would help to reduce the amount his body absorbed.

'Gary, I'm going to give you something to help your body get rid of the drugs still in your stomach. And I'm going to take a blood sample to see how you're doing.'

She took the sample, capped it and called to the staff nurse working on her team. 'Miche, can you get the bloods sorted, please? Usual stuff—full blood count, Us and Es, creatinine, glucose and arterial blood gases. And if you could give me a hand with some activated charcoal?'

'My favourite,' Michelle said wryly. 'I'll get these to the lab and then I'll come back.'

The charcoal was messy but effective.

'I'm not happy about his temperature—or his blood pressure,' Holly muttered to Michelle a little later.

'Or his ECG,' Michelle said, looking at the display. 'He's still tachycardic.'

Before either of them could say another word, Gary started having a fit.

'Oh, no. Can someone get me some chlormethiazole?' she called. Although diazepam was usually used to control fits, chlormethiazole had the extra benefit of helping to lower a fever.

'Hold his arm still for me. I'll get it in,' David said, appearing with a syringe.

'Sure,' Holly said, knowing that now wasn't the time to be proud. She needed his hands as well as the contents of the syringe. When someone was having an epileptic fit, it was much easier if one person held the arm still while another did the injection. Michelle was holding Gary's head, making sure he didn't swallow his tongue. Holly held Gary's arm still and David injected the chlormethiazole.

The fit stopped, and then Gary was sick again.

'It's OK,' Holly soothed, wiping his face. How many times had a doctor given the same treatment to her brother, back in Liverpool? And how many more times would it have to happen before Dan realised what an idiot he was being?

Gary couldn't be more than a year or two younger than her brother. For a moment her vision blurred and she saw Daniel's face in front of her. Then she blinked. Hard. This *wasn't* Dan. And her brother had been clean for months now. He might even have turned the corner.

And elephants were pink, with wings.

When Holly was sure that Gary was responding to his treatment, she almost staggered to the rest room for a break.

She nearly walked out again when she saw David already sitting there. She really, really wasn't in the mood for facing him right now.

'Hey.' Almost as if he'd guessed that she was about to back away, he held up a bar of chocolate. 'I owe you half, I think. Seeing as you shared your brownie with me last night.'

Colleagues. Yes. She could handle that.

She grabbed a coffee and sank into the chair next to his. 'Thanks,' she said, taking the proffered squares.

'Tough night?' he asked.

'Drug cases always get to me. I suppose it's because of Dan,' she said. 'I always think it could be him.'

'Why?'

She sighed. 'He got in with a bad crowd at uni and went off the rails pretty spectacularly. He's living with Mum and Dad right now, in a temporary truce—but every so often he does something stupid, Mum gets too heavy with him and I have to go back to broker peace between them again.'

'Little Danny does *drugs*?' Disbelief was written all over David's face.

'Dan's not so little now,' she said wryly. 'He's twenty-five—bigger than me. Bigger than you, actually.' She shrugged. 'Ah, well. Your mother was right. Our family's stuck-up, and we've had our comeuppance for it. Both of the kids brought shame on the family.'

'What do you mean?' he asked.

As if he didn't know. 'Forget it,' she said shortly.

'Holly—'

'Just forget it,' she said, and walked out before she said something she'd regret.

Just what was going on in her head? She was impossible. Really, really impossible, David thought angrily. Holly might be a good doctor—and good at defusing awkward situations with patients—but her manner with him left a hell of a lot to be desired. Yes, they had a history, but she shouldn't take out her guilt on him!

Maybe on Monday, after he'd had some sleep, he'd have a word with Sue and see if he could be moved to the other team.

'Peter Kirby. Suspected multiple rib fractures,' Rick said as he ran through the handover. 'Query organ damage, too.'

Holly glanced at their patient and winced. 'Someone's given him a hell of a kicking. Funny, he doesn't look the fighting type.'

'Probably just in the wrong place at the wrong time,' Rick said wryly. 'Wouldn't surprise me if it was gay-bashing.'

'Hey. We're not all homophobic,' she said gently, touching his arm. 'Do you know him?'

He rolled his eyes. 'I don't know *every* gay male in London.'

'What? A seasoned flirt like you?' Holly teased.

He grinned. 'Let's just say the old radar tells me something.'

'Be careful out there, yeah?' she asked.

'I can look after myself.'

It wasn't a macho boast. Rick had run self-defence classes for the staff last year, and was qualified in martial arts. 'You know what I mean.'

'Yeah, sugar. I know. Right, I'm going to do my reports. And then I'm going home to sleep, sleep, *sleep*.'

'I should be so lucky.' Holly smiled at him, then went over to her patient and introduced herself. 'I'm just going to examine you, Peter. I'll be as gentle as I can, but tell me if you need me to stop, OK?'

'My chest hurts,' he whispered. 'Hurts all over.'

'OK, Peter. I'll give you something to help that.' She inserted a couple of IV lines then gave him IV analgesics, noting as she did so that his breathing was a little faster than she would have liked and there were slight traces of blue round his lips, a condition known as cyanosis.

Which meant compromised respiration.

'Hurts to breathe,' he said.

It could be a tension pneumothorax, where air leaked into the space around the lungs and was trapped. The pressure caused one of the lungs to collapse and could rapidly lead to a cardiac arrest.

Then Holly noticed something she really, really hadn't wanted to see. As Peter breathed in, part of his chest moved inwards too, and as he breathed out the same segment moved out again. Flail chest, she thought with a sinking heart. Where at least three ribs had broken, in two or more places, part of the chest wall could move independently— known as 'flail chest', it meant that there was likely to be significant damage to the lung underneath it. If he got through surgery, he'd be in Intensive Care for a while.

A quick check on the pulse oximeter showed her that Peter's oxygen saturation was dropping. His blood pressure was low, too, so either it was a tension pneumothorax or there was a chance that the kicking he'd received had ruptured something, possibly his spleen.

'I'm going to put you on an oxygen mask,' she told him. 'That'll help you breathe more easily. Take it slowly—in and one and out and one,' she counted as she slipped the mask over his head. 'Miche, we need a chest X-ray and the usual bloods, cross-matching,' she said. She slipped on the earpieces to her stethoscope. 'Can you get David?'

David was at her side almost immediately. Holly turned away from Peter for a moment and gave David a quick run-down in a low voice. 'There's definitely flail chest but I don't know how bad the damage is. I'm not happy with his blood pressure or his oxygen sats. I don't think it's a tension pneumothorax—I've checked and there's no absence of breath sounds on one side, no tracheal deviation, and his neck veins aren't distended. I think the low BP could be related to organ damage rather than a tension pneumothorax.'

'Have you ordered a chest X-ray?'

'Yes, and the usual bloods.'

'OK. We'll get Theatre on standby and warn the anaesthetist there's a strong risk of pneumothorax,' David said. 'We need to find out if there's any internal bleeding. Any obvious signs?'

'No.'

'DPL, then.' Diagnostic peritoneal lavage, or DPL, was used in patients with multiple injuries to assess possible abdominal injuries. 'Can you get the patient's consent?'

Holly held Peter's hand and explained what they wanted to do and why. 'Can you sign a consent form for me, sweetheart?'

'Yeah,' he whispered.

The scrawl was barely decipherable but it was enough.

While David fitted a nasogastric tube, Holly inserted a catheter to decompress Peter's bladder. Holly cleaned Peter's skin while David draped sterile towels over the area, then gave Peter a local anaesthetic.

'Ready?' he said to Holly.

'Ready.' Strange how easily they'd gelled into a team, working together without getting in each other's way or even needing to say much to the other. But then, she'd known him so well, all those years ago. She'd almost been able to read his thoughts.

Which was why his behaviour had hurt so very much

when he'd let her down. Because it had been the last thing she'd expected.

David made a vertical incision in the skin, about three centimetres long. 'Can you put pressure on the edges, Hol?'

To minimise bleeding. 'OK.'

'Dividing the linea alba,' he said. To her relief, he was the type who said exactly what he was doing so she didn't have to second-guess him. 'I've got the peritoneum. Can I have clips, please?'

Holly was already passing them to him.

'Thanks.' David brought the peritoneum into the wound and felt the edge between his thumbs to check no bowel had been caught into the clips. When he was satisfied, he made a tiny incision and inserted a peritoneal dialysis catheter, made sure the seal was tight and aspirated the fluid.

'Positive,' Holly said very quietly as blood started to appear. 'He needs a laparotomy.'

'I'll close. You get Theatre,' David said.

While Peter was being whisked to Theatre, Holly and David cleared up in Resus.

'Thanks for your help,' Holly said. 'It's good to know I can rely on you…'

David frowned. Was it his imagination, or had she muttered 'now'? Her face said it, too. 'What do you mean, *now*?' he demanded.

She smiled thinly. 'You know exactly what I mean.'

'I think,' he said quietly, 'we need to talk.'

'The time for talking was twelve years ago. You weren't interested then—and I'm not interested now.'

'What?' His frown deepened. 'Hang on a minute. Twelve years ago you dumped me.'

She scoffed. 'More like you abandoned me. Just when I needed you.'

His eyes narrowed. 'I can't be hearing you straight. I

must be in caffeine withdrawal.' He glanced at his watch. 'Look, we're both at the end of our shifts. It's been a long night and we're both tired. Come and have breakfast with me. I just want a bacon sandwich—preferably with a ton of tomato ketchup.'

She shook her head. 'Forget it.'

'Hol, we need to talk.'

'I don't think your wife will be very happy about that.'

'I'm divorced. And, anyway, I'm only asking you to talk to me.' He paused. 'What about you? Anyone waiting at home who'd be worried if you were late?'

'No.'

'Then I think we owe it to each other to get this straightened out. If nothing else, it's going to be easier to work together. That, or I'm going to have to ask for a transfer to the other team because I can't work with you—not if there's all this stuff bubbling under the surface. Everybody knows you went to school with me. So what's the gossip machine going to claim when we can't work together?'

Holly sighed. 'All right. Breakfast it is—but not in the hospital canteen. There's a greasy spoon just down the road. It'll be quieter.'

'We need to do our handovers. Meet you in—' he glanced at his watch '—ten minutes?'

'By the entrance.'

'OK. And if anyone asks, we're simply colleagues flaking together after a heavy shift, in need of breakfast.'

They didn't speak as Holly led the way to the café. Not until David had ordered two bacon sandwiches with lots of ketchup and two large black coffees.

'I'm too tired to be polite. Let's cut to the chase,' he said as they sat down at a table at the back of the café. 'Where do you get this ''abandon'' thing from?'

'I can understand why you did it. Typical teenage boy. Can't face telling his girl it's over, so he doesn't ring her, doesn't contact her, doesn't return any of her calls—and if she's pushy he gets his mum to tell her it's over.'

He snorted. 'Rubbish! More like you'd finished slumming it and you got *your* mum to tell me it was over. And don't lie, Hol. You didn't return any of my calls.'

'What calls?'

'Come on. I must have phoned you dozens of times, and every time you got your mum to say you were out. When you didn't turn up to take your A levels, I asked Mrs Smith what had happened to you.' Their old biology teacher. 'She was in the exam room. She told me you'd arranged to take your exams somewhere else.'

She frowned. 'Yes.'

David's lip curled. 'So you'd had it planned for God knows how long.'

'No. It was a last-minute thing.'

He scoffed. 'Come off it. You can't change your exam centre at the last minute.'

'Yes, you can.' Holly lifted her chin. 'Mum organised it. I suppose she knew who to talk to.'

Yeah, well. Laura Jones *would*. She'd probably been mates with the chairman of the examining board.

His thoughts must have been written all over his face, because Holly folded her arms defensively. 'But there was a good reason for it.'

'Such as?'

'If you remember so much about it, then you'll also remember there was something else worrying me besides exams.'

'You were stressed, yes.'

'Oh, for goodness' sake! Do I have to spell it out?'

She'd dumped him, and now she was trying to claim it had been the other way round. 'Yes, Holly. You do.'

'I'd missed two periods.'

'You told me it was exam nerves, because the same thing had happened just before your GCSEs. And you were a vir—' He exhaled sharply, as if someone had just thumped him in the stomach. Hard.

Holly had been a virgin before he'd met her. When their relationship had progressed to making love they'd been careful, but condoms weren't a hundred per cent reliable. His head started spinning. Was she telling him…?

'Oh, my God.' He couldn't get any air into his lungs. 'Are you telling me we've…we've got a child?' He stared at her in disbelief. 'I've got a son or daughter who's—' he calculated the age quickly '—about eleven years old?' How could she have kept a secret like *that* from him? How could she possibly have had his child and not told him?

Holly shook her head. 'You don't have a child, David.'

'All right. So you didn't name me as the father.' But no way could the father have been anyone else. Holly might have dropped him without bothering to tell him it was over, but she'd been faithful to him while they'd been together. He was sure of that without having to ask. But he had to know the truth. Did they have a child? '*Are* you telling me that you have a child who is eleven years old?' he asked, his voice shaking slightly.

'No.'

'Then what? You had the baby adopted?' Her mother would have put pressure on her. A lot of pressure. Of course Holly would have caved in. Nobody could withstand Laura Jones in full flow.

'No.'

He stared at her. She couldn't have… She wouldn't have… Surely not. Not even if her mother had frogmarched her to a private clinic somewhere…would she? 'You had a termination?' he asked, his mouth dry.

'I had a miscarriage,' she informed him quietly. 'It started two hours before I was going to sit my first exam. I was in hospital for two days. So I didn't take my A levels at all that year. I had a gap year and sat them the following summer.'

'You had a miscarriage?' Even though her eyes were telling him to back off, he needed to touch her. Comfort her. Feel her touch comforting him. They'd lost a baby and he'd had no idea. He reached across the table and took her hands. 'Hol, I'm so, so sorry. I had no idea. If I'd known, or even guessed…I would have been right there with you. I'd have sat by your bedside and held your hand, and to hell with my exams.'

She withdrew her hands. 'Yeah, right. You cared that much.'

'You know I did. I loved you, Holly. More than anyone.' Before—or since. Not that she needed to know that. 'Your mum said you didn't want to speak to me. I didn't believe her, so I waited outside your house, hoping I'd get a chance to see you. You were in the car with your mum. And you blanked me.'

'What did you expect? David, I'd just had a miscarriage. I couldn't take my exams so I lost my place at university, and my career plans had gone down the toilet. And, worst of all, my so-called boyfriend couldn't even be bothered to return my calls.'

'I *did* ring you. Several times.'

'Right. And that's why you went on holiday with another girl?'

'I did *what*?'

'When I… Afterwards.' She gulped and David suddenly realised how much it must have affected her. Maybe that was the reason why the sweet Holly Jones he'd once known had become so hard. Since she'd lost their baby and thought he'd deserted her.

'When I thought I could face you without crying, I went round to your place. Your mum was there on her own. She said you'd gone on holiday, with another girl.'

None of this made sense. Had he just been transported to some weird parallel universe? 'Don't be stupid. She wouldn't say something like that.'

'You're calling me a liar?' She folded her arms. 'You weren't there. It was the week after the exams finished.'

He thought back and frowned. 'I went on holiday, yes.'

'With another girl.'

'What? That's ridiculous. I nearly cracked up, what with you dumping me just before the exams. So my uncle David—my mum's brother, the one I was named after—took me on holiday to get me out of the house and try to stop me moping around.'

'Your mum said you'd gone with another girl.'

'You must have misunderstood. I went with my aunt and uncle, and my little cousin Jeannie.'

Holly made a contemptuous noise. 'Your mother was very clear about it. She said you'd gone on holiday with your girlfriend. She didn't mention your aunt or uncle. She lied to me, David.'

He shook his head. 'She wouldn't have done that.'

Holly took a swig of coffee. 'Wake up, will you? Your mum hated me. She'd have done anything to keep us apart. Did she tell you that I came round?'

'Well, no,' he admitted.

'She wanted to make sure I stayed away from you.'

He frowned. 'As far as she was concerned, you'd dumped me. You broke my heart, Hol. She was probably trying to protect me and make sure you didn't hurt me again.'

She laughed mirthlessly. 'Your loyalty's commendable. It's just a shame you didn't show the same loyalty to me when I needed it.'

'That's unfair. I didn't know about the baby.'

'And your mother was wrong. I didn't dump you. Of *course* I bloody didn't! I rang you to tell you I'd done a pregnancy test.'

'I didn't get the message.'

'I spoke to your mother. I didn't tell her what the problem was—I wasn't *that* stupid—just that I needed to talk to you. But she said you were out.'

He shrugged. 'I probably was.'

'So why didn't you ring me back?'

'Because I didn't get the message.'

'Deliberately.'

'It might have slipped her mind.'

She shook her head. 'No way.'

He sighed. 'If, and I mean *if* it was deliberate, she did it with the best of intentions. What about your mother? She said you were in but you just didn't want to talk to me. Her exact words were that you couldn't be *bothered* with me.'

Holly scoffed. 'She knew I loved you. She knew about the baby. What reason would she have to lie to you?'

'Because she didn't like me, and you know it. She was perfectly nice when she met me, until she found out I didn't have a dad and I lived on a council estate. I wasn't the right social class for you and she probably didn't want her daughter having a kid with someone who didn't know— oh, the difference between a Burgundy glass and a Chablis glass.'

Holly used a word that her mother definitely wouldn't have appreciated.

It was enough to break the tension. David laughed.

'What's so funny?' she demanded.

'I can just imagine your mother's face if she was sitting here right now and heard what you just said.'

'She's past all that. What with one kid unmarried and pregnant at eighteen and the other a drug addict who's supposedly in rehab but can't quite stay clean...' Holly shrugged. 'The odd bit of swearing doesn't bother her nowadays.'

'I didn't dump you, Holly,' he said quietly. 'I had no idea you were expecting our baby.'

The silence stretched between them until David thought that every window in the café was going to implode.

And then she spoke. Very quietly. 'And if you'd known the truth?'

Her eyes were guarded. Mistrustful. Was it his imagination, or was there a tiny spark of longing, too? Of yearning for what might have been?

There was only one thing he could say. The truth. 'I'd have been at your side. All the way.'

Their bacon sandwiches arrived, effectively stopping Holly's reply.

They ate in silence, though every mouthful felt as if it was choking him. Holly had been expecting their baby. She'd lost their baby the day of her first exam. And their parents had leapt on the chance to stop a relationship they'd disapproved of—her mother because he wasn't good enough, and his mother because she'd thought Holly was too posh.

They'd never stood a chance.

In the end he pushed his sandwich away, half-eaten. 'So where do we go from here?'

The question hung in the air.

Eventually, she sighed. 'I don't know.'

'Do you want me to ask Sue to switch one of us to another team?'

'Yes. No.' She sighed. 'I'm tired, David. It's been a long night.'

And they'd both had a shock. 'We need time to think about it. After a good sleep.' Not that he thought he *could* sleep, after the bombshell she'd dropped.

'Yeah.' She gave up on her sandwich, too.

'Come on. I'll walk you home. Maybe we can talk later, when we're both feeling a bit less fragile.'

She lifted her chin. 'I don't need you to walk me home.'

'I know. But it'd make me feel better,' he admitted. It was the least he could do—considering he hadn't been there for her when she'd really needed him. Even though he'd had no idea at the time.

For a moment he thought she was going to refuse. But then she nodded. 'OK.'

They walked in silence back to Holly's house. 'Can I call you later?' he asked.

'OK. Got a pen?'

'Mmm-hmm.' He clicked a ballpoint pen and stood poised to write her number on the back of his hand. Then he became aware that she was laughing.

'What?'

'You still do that? Scribble notes on your hand because otherwise you'll forget or lose the bit of paper?'

'Old habits die hard,' he said lightly.

'Hmm.' She gave him her number.

'I'll call you. And, Holly?'

She turned back from her unlocked front door. 'What?'

'I'm sorry. I should have been braver. I should have faced your mother at your door and demanded to see you.'

She shook her head. 'You were only eighteen—and my mother's scary.'

If the other staff were to be believed, Holly was rapidly turning into a woman just as scary as Laura Jones.

Except Holly had a soft centre. And he must be seriously sleep-deprived even to consider trying to find it again.

CHAPTER FOUR

'YOU sound rough,' Judith said when Holly answered the phone.

'I've just done two nights. Friday *and* Saturday,' Holly pointed out.

'You're supposed to go to sleep all day Sunday, set your alarm for five o'clock and then do something nice. Want to come and see a movie with me and Zo? I'll even buy the popcorn.'

'Movie. Hmm. Are we talking slush, action or sci-fi?'

Judith chuckled. 'It's a comedy.'

Holly groaned, knowing exactly what that meant in her best friend's terms. The kind of film that Holly absolutely loathed. 'No. Not even if you give me a whole box of gianduja.' Gianduja, a mixture of toasted hazelnuts and cocoa butter shaped into little cubes, had long been a favourite with Holly—and Judith had been the one to introduce her to it. 'Thanks for the offer, Jude, but I'm going to have a run, then a long bath and a night watching reruns of *The X-Files*.'

'Well, I can't compete with David, can I?' Judith teased.

'David?' Oh, no. Don't say the gossip machine had started already. Holly's heart missed a beat.

'You really are in nights mode, aren't you? *David*. You know—Mr Duchovny? The actor you've been drooling over for years and years?'

'Oh. Yes.'

Concern deepened Judith's voice. 'You sure you're OK,

Holls? Zo thought you seemed a bit flat at Giovanni's the other night.'

'I'm fine,' Holly reassured her. 'But thanks for asking.'

'So how's the new boy?'

'New boy?'

'The one you told us was starting this week. The job Zo tried to get you to go for, except you were being a stubborn old bat and decided it wasn't the right time for you.'

'Oh, him.' Now was the time when she should tell Jude everything. And Zoe. Maybe she should go out with them tonight—if she let her bombshell drop before the film, they'd end up dropping the film and going out for a meal. Preferably in an ice-cream café. And her best friends would definitely talk some sense into her.

But then she'd have to explain why she hadn't trusted them—why she hadn't told them about the baby.

Zoe would understand. She'd kept a tender secret of her own for years. But Holly didn't want to hurt her best friends. And until she'd sorted things out in her head, she'd only make a mess of telling them. 'He's all right.' She yawned. 'Uh. I need coffee. Or ice cream.'

'We can do ice cream. And popcorn. Salted, not sweet.'

Holly's favourite, not theirs. If Judith had been standing in front of her, Holly would have hugged her. Hard. 'Yeah, and I know the price. A slushy film. Nah. You and Zo enjoy it. Go and be completely wet together. And don't forget your tissues—it's not nice to wipe your nose on your sleeve.'

'You horrible woman,' Judith said, but she was laughing. 'I'll see you for lunch on Thursday, then. Usual time, usual place.'

'As long as you don't have an emergency delivery, Zo's clinic doesn't overrun and we're not up to our eyes in ED— you bet.'

'Enjoy your days off. And don't spend *all* of them in front of the telly.'

'As if,' Holly teased back.

Holly had just changed into a T-shirt that had seen better days, an old pair of tracksuit bottoms and her running shoes when the doorbell went.

She frowned. She wasn't expecting callers. Unless Dan had had another spat with their parents and flounced off to London to calm down.

Right now, she wasn't in the mood for her kid brother. Particularly if he was in brat mode. And if it was someone trying to cold-call her, they'd get very short shrift. She flung the front door open, about to lambaste whoever had just rung her doorbell—and stopped.

David was standing there, holding a huge bunch of bright orange gerberas.

She blinked. Was this a mirage?

No. He was still there. With flowers.

'Peace offering,' he said.

Her eyes narrowed. 'I thought you were going to ring me?'

'I was. Then I thought I'd rather do this face to face,' he admitted.

'You look terrible.'

'Probably because I didn't sleep very well. I've been thinking.'

'Me too,' she said wryly. She stood aside. 'Come in. Um—do you want a coffee?'

'Thanks. If it's no trouble.'

How had it come to this? They'd loved each other. Lost each other. And now they were pussyfooting round each other like strangers. 'It's no trouble.'

'I'm not interrupting anything?'

'Nothing that can't wait.'

He followed her into the kitchen, still carrying the flowers. 'Wow. I didn't expect you to go for monochrome.'

Holly glanced round at the white walls, granite work-surface and plain white units. 'What, then?'

'Flowers and chintzy stuff.'

She pulled a face. 'Don't confuse my taste with my mother's.'

'No,' he said dryly, handing her the flowers.

She unwrapped them, filled a huge blue glass vase with water and arranged the gerberas quickly and professionally. 'Thank you for these. They're lovely.'

'Best I could find on a Sunday evening.'

'They're still lovely. Nice, uncomplicated lines. Not fussy or frilly. And they brighten up my kitchen.' She placed the flowers on the window-sill, switched the kettle on and tipped coffee into a cafetière. When she'd made the coffee, she ushered him through into the living room.

It had the same plain lines as the kitchen—white walls, wooden floors, two deep red sofas, a state-of-the-art sound system and a floor-to-ceiling unit housing her CDs. Again, David had half expected chintz and flounces. But even the painting on the wall had clean lines: a large, bold, bright abstract, framed very simply. Nothing like the country scenes in fussy gilt frames on the walls of her parents' house.

He sat on one of the sofas. True to form, Holly took the other, sitting opposite him rather than next to him. Well. He could deal with this. They were going to sort things out between them once and for all.

He took a sip of coffee. 'This is good stuff, Hol.'

'Italian.' She eyed him over the rim of her mug. 'So what did you really want?'

'Just to talk.' He'd been thinking about it all day.

Wondering about all the might-have-beens. The words tumbled out before he could stop them. 'I can't believe we made a baby.'

'Get over it, David. I have.'

Something in the roughness of her voice alerted him. 'Have you? *Really*, I mean?'

She didn't answer.

'It's not that far off what we planned—just a bit earlier.' He stared into his coffee. 'We could have worked it out, deferred our places at university. If we'd taken a gap year together while you were pregnant and had the baby, I could have got a job and earned some money to tide us over. We could have got a little place together in Southampton the following October, found a good childminder and worked out a schedule so we could both study and share looking after the baby. It would have been hard work, but we could have done it. Together.'

When she didn't say a word, he looked up. Then he realised she was crying. Not loudly—far worse than that. She was weeping silently. Tears were running down her face and she was making no attempt to stop them.

'Hol?'

'That's what I—' She stopped, and scrubbed at her eyes.

'What?' he asked gently. Was that what she'd hoped for, too?

When she spoke, her voice had hardened again. 'David, it's all in the past. I had a miscarriage. We didn't have a baby. So there's no point in speculating on might-have-beens.'

'So where do we go from here?'

She shrugged. 'We're colleagues.'

'Can you handle working with me?'

'Can *you* handle working with *me*?' she retorted.

'Yes. I think.' He sighed. 'I didn't come here to hector

you. It's just… Part of my life I thought was over…well, it isn't.'

'Yes, it is.'

'I've spent the past twelve years believing a lie, Hol. So have you. And now everything's all mixed up again.'

'It doesn't change a thing.'

Didn't it? Or was she just too scared to look at the possibilities?

Not that there was any point in asking. Holly had a reputation for being scary, not scared. No way would she admit to a single weakness. Instead, he changed tack. 'Tell me about what happened to you—after that summer.'

She shrugged. 'There isn't much to tell. I went to a different college to sit my A levels. I passed, got an offer to study in London, trained here—and then I applied for the SHO's post in the emergency department. Sue promoted me last year.'

'You've done well.' He paused. 'I never expected to find you here. I thought you'd be in a little practice somewhere in the country—in a nice part of Cheshire, or something. You were going to be a GP.'

'So were you.'

'When I qualified, my heart wasn't in it any more,' he admitted. 'I wanted something where I wouldn't have to—' He stopped.

'Where you wouldn't have to get involved?'

She'd read his mind. Just as she'd always been able to— before they'd been wrenched apart. Or was it that…? 'It was the same for you, wasn't it?' he asked softly.

She nodded. 'And it worked.'

'For me, too. Until you walked in last Monday morning.' He took another sip of coffee. 'So what about socially? You're not married.'

'We've already established that. And that you're divorced. Serious girlfriend?'

He shook his head. 'Serious boyfriend?'

'No.'

'Why not?'

'I'm busy with my career. Actually, I had thought about applying for the senior reg's job.'

He flinched. 'So I took your job as well?'

She shook her head. 'No. I knew I didn't have enough experience, so I didn't even apply for it. I'm a year behind you, remember? But, yes, my next move's a senior reg post in emergency medicine. Preferably at London City General, because I love it here.'

'So you want me to stick around for a year before I give up and let you have my job?'

Her face grew shuttered. 'I didn't say that.'

'I was teasing you, Hol,' he said softly. 'Lighten up.'

She bit her lip. 'Yeah. Sorry. I, um, suffer from rideo-myopathy.'

He translated mentally. A weak sense of humour? Underused, perhaps—but she was clever. Very clever. Had wit enough to make a joke like that in Latin, turning it into a cod-medical term.

Except what he wanted to talk about was no joke.

He set his empty mug on the floor, then joined her on her sofa, ignoring the wariness in her face. He didn't want to say this with too much space between them. 'Hol, I rang my mum today.'

There was a beat before she answered. 'And?'

'I told her I'd met you again.'

'Oh.'

He took her hand. 'I asked her why she did it. Why she lied to you—and to me.'

'Was I right?'

'Yep.'

Silence stretched between them. But at least she didn't shake off his hand. The weird thing was, this felt right. More right than his three-year marriage to Alyson, the marriage that had broken down irretrievably before he'd gone to Newcastle.

Holding Holly's hand felt like coming home.

Which was stupid. Because no way were they going to pick up where they'd left off. They couldn't. They were different people. Older. Wiser. Wanted different things.

Or did they?

'Guess what?' she said.

'You did the same?'

'Sort of.' She wrinkled her nose. 'Mum was out—some fundraising thing or other.'

'So you don't know?'

'Yes, I do. I asked Dad.'

'And?'

'You were right, too.'

He smiled thinly. 'The country's crying out for good GPs. And, between them, our mums managed to blitz two potential GPs before they even started training.'

'That's a bit unfair. Once we'd started training, we might have found out we liked the buzz of emergency medicine more than the little country idyll we had planned,' she pointed out. 'And, actually, I like living in London.'

'I think the country would spook me. Too quiet, too dark at night,' David admitted.

'So it was Southampton, Newcastle and here?'

'SHO at Southampton. Then I got divorced and a registrar's post came up at Newcastle. It felt like a good idea at the time, and I liked the place. A lot.'

'What was she like?'

'Who?'

'Your wife.'

'Alyson? Tall, blonde hair, brown eyes.' As opposite from Holly as he could find. Except, if he was honest about it, he'd never been able to get his first love completely out of his mind. 'She worked in PR. I met her when we were students—she's a couple of years younger than I am. We got married after I qualified and she graduated. But a junior doctor's social life doesn't quite mesh with the rest of the world's. I didn't want to party until three in the morning the night before I was on an early, and I think she got fed up with my job. Weekend shifts and long hours meant we couldn't go to stay with people; night duty meant she was on her own too much. So she tried to persuade me to be a media doctor instead. She had the contacts. She could have got me a slot on the radio, a syndicated column in a couple of papers, an advice page in a couple of magazines. But I like treating people, not pieces of paper.'

He sighed. 'In the end, we realised it wasn't going to work and we called it quits.' He gave her a sidelong glance. 'What about you?'

'Like you say, a doctor's social hours don't fit in with anyone who's not a medic.'

So had there been someone serious, or not? Something in her eyes warned him not to push too hard. And to release her hand.

'Have you eaten yet?' she asked.

'No.'

'Want to stay for dinner? As a peace offering,' she added.

'I'd like that. Anything I can do to help?'

'Depends. Can you cook?'

David rolled his eyes. 'Do you think all men are useless, or just me?'

'Now, *that's* a leading question.'

He collected his empty mug and followed her into the kitchen. 'What do you want me to do?'

'Do you eat curry—and chicken?'

Once, she wouldn't have had to ask. But it had been so long that they barely knew anything about each other.

'Yes, to both.'

'Good.' She rummaged in the fridge, then handed him a pile of vegetables. 'Can you slice that lot for me? I need the tomatoes skinned and chopped.'

'Sure.'

While he chopped, Holly heated oil in a pan, shook in some spices and started sealing the diced chicken breasts. 'There's some naan bread in the freezer,' she said, when he added the chopped vegetables to the pan.

Cooking with Holly felt...*weird*, he decided. It was something they'd never had the chance to do when they'd been going out together. But he liked it. Teamwork.

Hell. They would have been so *good* together. If he'd married Holly, it wouldn't have ended in divorce. They'd have had four kids and a dog and a cat and a hamster. She'd have taught their children to make biscuits, not caring how much flour they scattered everywhere. And having people dropping in unannounced at any time wouldn't have bothered her, the way it had Alyson—because it wouldn't have been for show, designed to help her image. With Holly, people would just have been drawn there.

Except... Holly Jones scared people away. Her house was very much a single person's house. Everything neat and in its place.

The past and present and might-have-beens blurred, and David wasn't sure which was which.

Maybe he just needed some sleep.

A short while later, Holly split the curry between two

plates, added the naan bread to a third and handed him two plates to carry through to her dining room.

'White walls again?' he asked as he set the plates on the table.

'Off-white, actually. But I like light spaces. I know it's trendy to do retro colours in period homes, but I couldn't live with dark red or sludge-green.'

She tells it like it is. Anna was dead right about that. David suppressed a smile. 'Actually, it's nice.' He joined her at the dining table, noticing the state-of-the-art computer equipment at the small table in the corner. 'Flash computer.'

She shrugged. 'A flat screen takes up less space.'

'So, are you working on a paper?'

'Not exactly.'

Getting information out of Holly could be like pulling teeth. A far cry from the gentle, sweet girl who'd been open about everything. Well. Nearly everything, he amended mentally. 'What, then?'

'I'd like to work in rapid response. So I'm taking a course in my spare time.'

'Impressive.'

'No. If you want to do something, you have to make it happen. It's not going to be handed to you out of thin air just because you want it.'

'True.' He took a mouthful of the curry. 'Hol, this is excellent.'

'Low in fat, high on taste.'

He raised an eyebrow. Holly wasn't rail-thin, but neither was she overweight. 'You don't need to diet.'

'No. But I also don't want to clog my arteries. Jude's a junk-food addict—well, she was—so this was my way of compensating. For too much pizza, that is.'

'Jude?'

'She's a registrar in Maternity.'

'You trained together?' he guessed.

'With Zo—she of the chocolate brownies. Zo's in Paeds.'

'And they're your best friends?'

'What is this, twenty questions?'

'No. Just making conversation.' He spotted her running machine in the corner of the room and switched to what he hoped was a safer topic. 'So why the treadmill?'

'Post-shift tension-buster.'

'Right.' He could understand that. It was the reason why he went swimming, doing lap after lap of front crawl until he felt ready to face the world again. 'You don't like the gym?'

'No. I used to run in the park round the corner.'

'And you got sick of being soaked in the rain?'

'No. I was mugged,' she said, matter-of-factly.

'Mugged?' Someone had hurt Holly—*his* Holly? His fists balled reflexively.

She rolled her eyes. 'Chill out, David. It's not a big deal. Rick—as in our paramedic Rick—ran some self-defence classes last year and made every woman in the ED learn a few moves.' She gave him a wicked smile. 'Actually, I felt a bit sorry for the mugger. Apparently, I was his first target. And I had to take him to the ED. He broke his coccyx.'

How could a mugger have broken the little tailbone at the base of the spine?

The question must have been obvious in his face, because she explained, 'I threw him and he landed badly.' She shrugged. 'And then I upset his dignity a bit more. I'd gone running before my shift, instead of after. They were very, very busy in ED. So I was the doctor who diagnosed the problem.'

David knew exactly what she meant: diagnosing a broken coccyx wasn't done by a routine X-ray but by a rectal examination. Definitely adding insult to injury, in the mugger's eyes. 'Please, tell me you didn't show him that epidural kit before you offered him analgesics.'

She batted her eyelashes. '*Moi?* Well, his coccyx needed manipulation under local anaesthetic. He needed to know what I was going to do. I just demonstrated how I'd use a syringe. I didn't say it was the actual syringe I was going to use…'

David shook his head, smiling. 'I almost feel sorry for him.'

Holly smiled back. 'I think it taught him a lesson. The police had a little chat with him, and I doubt if he's tried mugging anyone again.'

'But it put you off the park?'

'No.' She grimaced. 'Jude and Zo found out about it through the grapevine. I suppose it was a pretty good story, so it was bound to spread. But they had a hissy fit and gave me an ultimatum: find something safer, or they'd tell my mum. The options were joining a gym or buying a treadmill. I want to run on my terms, not wait in a queue for the machine I want or have to work round opening hours that don't fit my shifts. And I'd rather run to music I like, not the stuff they play at most of the gyms—hence the treadmill.'

He grinned. 'They threatened you with your mum. Does anyone else in ED know?'

'No. And if they find out, I may get very nervous the next time you come anywhere near me—I might think you're a mugger and throw you.'

'And break my coccyx?' He chuckled. 'Point taken.'

They'd slipped so easily into teasing banter. And David thought he rather liked this new Holly. Feisty, not afraid to stick up for herself, and she was clearly very close to the two doctors who'd trained with her.

Maybe...

'What?'

His eyes widened. Had she just heard his thoughts? She'd skin him alive.

'Sorry?'

'You had a funny look on your face just then.'

'Did I?'

'What were you thinking?'

Sleep deprivation. Definitely sleep deprivation. Because completely the wrong thing came out. 'I was just thinking about kissing you.'

CHAPTER FIVE

WHY, why, why had he said something so stupid?

It had all been going so well. He and Holly were spending time together, putting the past behind them. They'd cooked dinner together. They were even laughing together.

And he'd blown it. Spectacularly. Any moment now she was going to ask him to leave.

So he'd go before he was pushed. Regroup. And work out a damage limitation strategy, starting tomorrow morning. 'I'm sorry. I'll, um, get out of your hair. Thanks for dinner. And I'm sorry.' All the apologies in the world didn't seem enough.

Holly still didn't say anything. David had got to the doorway when he heard her ask, very softly, 'Why do you want to kiss me?'

Heat zinged through his body. She was supposed to go ballistic and refuse to have anything to do with him, wasn't she? But, instead, she wanted to know why.

So maybe, just maybe, he hadn't blown it.

He turned round. Faced her. 'Because,' he said, equally softly, 'I like you, Holly Jones.'

'I'm not the naïve teenager you used to know,' she warned.

'I realise that. I like the woman you've become.' And I've never really stopped thinking about you. Wondering what went wrong. Wishing. Most of the time I kept you in the back of my mind, but you were always there. Waiting.

'I really hated you, David. For ruining my life. At the time I thought the world had ended. But it hasn't been

66

entirely bad. If I hadn't come here, I wouldn't have met Jude or Zo. I wouldn't have found a job I love. I wouldn't have had the space to become who I am.'

'I hated you, too. I didn't go out with anyone for three years after you.'

She didn't answer that, and jealousy nagged at him. Had Holly gone from man to man, seeking the love she'd thought he hadn't given her? Or had she become so choosy that she'd never gone out with anyone again?

Either way, it wasn't good. They'd hurt each other. Badly.

Now perhaps it was time to heal each other.

'You're single now?' she asked.

Did that mean she was going to give him another chance? He was having difficulty breathing. 'Yes. And you?'

'Yes.'

'Hol…' Words weren't enough. They weren't nearly enough to explain how he felt. What he wanted. What he needed.

Slowly, not quite believing that it was happening, he walked back over to her. Then she was in his arms, and he was kissing her as if he'd been starved of love for the last twelve years.

When he broke the kiss, they were both shaking.

'I didn't intend to leap on you.'

'Nor me.'

'Hol.' He stroked her face. 'I don't think I ever really got over you. And I know we're different people, now…but…' When she looked at him like that, he was lost. Completely lost. Unable to finish his sentence, he bent his head again. Kissed her until he was dizzy.

'I don't do relationships,' Holly told him when he broke the kiss.

'Neither do I.' He couldn't think straight. Not when she'd untucked his T-shirt from the waistband of his jeans and was stroking his skin like that.

'I don't do affairs either.'

'No.' He kissed her again. 'Uh. What was I saying?'

'I don't know.'

She looked as dazed as he felt. Good. So they were both in this together.

'Can I see you again?'

'We're both on early shift, as of Thursday morning,' she reminded him dryly.

'No. I mean outside work. Tomorrow. I want to spend the day with you. Go out somewhere.'

Her eyes narrowed. 'Are you asking me out?'

'Yes. You asked me why I wanted to kiss you. It's because I find you attractive, Holly. All of you. You're bright and you're beautiful and I want you. Right now, there's nothing I'd like more than to carry you straight to your bed and keep you there,' he admitted. 'But that wouldn't be fair to either of us. I don't want to rush you.'

She said nothing.

'But I do want to see you. Get to know you. See where it takes us this time round.' He punctuated every sentence with a kiss. 'Maybe we can give each other a second chance. Will you spend the day with me tomorrow?'

The sensible answer would have been no. But she'd gone past being sensible when she'd kissed him back. 'Let's take it slowly. No rush, no pressure.'

'No pressure,' he agreed. He nuzzled her cheek. 'So shall I meet you here?'

'Fine. What time?'

'Half past nine?'

She nodded.

'I'll help you with the washing-up before I go.'

'No need. There isn't that much.'

His mouth teased hers. 'Then I'll go now. Before my head gets overruled by another part of my anatomy.'

She smiled. 'Men.'

'Women,' he teased back.

She stroked his face. 'Until we're sure we know where this is going, I'd rather keep it quiet. I don't want the whole hospital talking about us.'

'Of course.' He captured her hand, pressed a kiss into her palm and folded her fingers over it. 'Until tomorrow. Half past nine.'

He was actually five minutes early. So he'd changed, Holly thought. As a teenager, he'd always been late until she'd surreptitiously altered his watch by five minutes.

No flowers. That suited her fine. It meant he wasn't going to be soppy or showy about things. No big gestures.

Though he looked good. More than good. Stone-coloured chinos, a black long-sleeved T-shirt to stave off the first chills of September in London, and a pair of very dark glasses. He could almost have been a film star on his day off.

She squashed the thought. Right now she needed to keep her libido under control. It had been too, too long since she'd done anything like this. Gone out with a man who made her feel like this, with her heart beating way too fast and her fingers tingling with adrenaline and shivers running down her spine.

She took a deep breath. 'Hi.'

'Ready?'

'Sure.' She set the burglar alarm and locked the house. 'Where are we going?'

'Depends what you want to do. We could go to

Hampstead for a walk on the heath, or do something cultural, or go shopping.'

Holly snorted. 'Do I look like a woman who enjoys shopping? I do most of mine over the Internet. In, click, and done with it. I only ever go with Jude and Zo if it's life-or-death stuff.' Like bridesmaids' dresses.

'OK. No shopping.'

David was trying to be nice. But he was definitely having problems suppressing a smile. Holly gave him a speculative look. 'How about,' she whispered, 'we do something really, really…?'

'What?'

She'd just bet his eyes were glittering behind his dark glasses. Glittering with excitement and hope and…

Take it steady, she reminded herself. 'Let's go and see some sharks.'

'Sharks?'

'Yeah. Big things. Live in the ocean. Scary teeth. And more people were killed by hamster bites than by sharks in the US last year.'

'No way.'

'I can't remember the exact figures,' she admitted. 'But it was something like that. Sharks get an unfair press.'

'For being scary? Maybe they're not the only ones.' David grinned back. 'You're on.'

They spent the morning wandering around the London Aquarium. Holly was particularly taken by the rays.

'They fascinate me. There's a sea-life centre near Brandham that has rays and about ten different sorts of jellyfish.'

'Where's Brandham?'

'On the Norfolk coast—a couple of hours north from here. Zo's aunt has a cottage near Brandham,' she explained. 'I've stayed there with Zo and Jude a few times.

One time we went, it did nothing but rain. We managed to persuade Zo out of the idea of going for a paddle and we went to the sea-life centre instead. There's this tunnel where you can walk through the sharks and see them swimming all around you, and then a stingray suddenly goes over your head. You can feed the rays there, too.'

'Which *you* obviously did.'

'I bought some ray food, but the others flatly refused to touch dead fish.' She sighed. 'Wimps. So I had to do all of it. Though I must admit, rays don't have very nice faces when they pop up out of the water for their dinner.'

David slid his arm round her shoulders. 'Nothing scares you, does it?'

'Not any more.' She'd already faced demons, lost the love of her life and her baby. Nothing else could be that bad.

His arm tightened. 'I'm sorry.'

'Hey. This is meant to be looking forward to see what happens. Not looking back at water that passed under the bridge so long ago that it's evaporated.'

But somehow, as they walked round the aquarium, her arm ended up round his waist. It felt so familiar…and so right. She'd expected some kind of awkwardness between them, at least this first time. But there wasn't. It was as if the past twelve years and all the heartache had never happened.

And *that*, she thought, was really scary.

Finally, they went to see the sharks. 'Being a medic, I ought to say that the nurse shark's my favourite,' Holly said. 'But I like the tiger sharks best.'

'They suit you. Scary.' He bared his teeth at her.

She laughed. 'Did you know that the most common name for a goldfish—in the UK, at least—is Jaws?'

'I'm not even going to ask how you know that. Do you come here often, Dr Jones?'

'Whatever gives you that idea, Dr Neave?' she teased back.

They had lunch at a small café overlooking the Thames.

'We've just been to see the sharks. You were practically cooing over the terrapins and the rays. And now you're ordering *fish* for lunch?' David asked in mock horror when Holly had chosen from the menu.

'I happen to like swordfish. Though I don't eat it that often because of the mercury levels.' She smiled at him. 'But I've been here before and the food's excellent. They do the best Greek salad ever.'

Good food, a glass of red wine and the early autumn sunshine put them both in a mellow mood, and they spent the afternoon wandering around the South Bank. Finally, they ended up at Holly's house.

'Thanks for today. I've really enjoyed it.' David smiled at her. 'I don't want it to end. But I'm not going to pressure you.'

'You can come in, if you want to.'

'I don't trust myself. And I want to keep my coccyx in one piece.'

Holly laughed. 'I wish I hadn't told you that story.'

'Someone else would've done. It's a classic.' His smile faded. 'Hol. Can I see you again? Outside work, I mean.'

She nodded. But when he leaned forward to kiss her, she took a step back.

Hurt flickered across his face. 'Sorry. I promised not to rush you.'

'I just don't want an audience,' Holly explained. 'My neighbours are…let's say, they're attentive.'

David glanced behind him and saw a lace curtain drop into place.

'That's Mrs Smith,' Holly said dryly. 'We, um, had rather a public proposal of marriage around here not so long ago. It's given everyone ideas.'

'Right. So a peck on the cheek would be misconstrued?'

Particularly when it turned out to be rather more than a peck on the cheek, Holly thought. 'Yes.'

'See you Thursday, then.' He'd put the sunglasses back in place so she couldn't see his eyes.

'Bright and early in Resus,' she promised.

Not that Holly had a chance to say more than hello to David on Thursday morning. One of her first cases, Melvyn Platt, was a serious one.

'I feel such a fool. And I'm probably wasting your time, but the wife threw a hissy fit and brought me here,' he said with a grimace.

'He was playing squash on Saturday morning and got a ball in the eye,' Melvyn's wife explained. 'His partner had to drive him home because he couldn't see. Double vision. And he's still got it. Leave it to him and he'll wait until he's completely blind before he'll even see a doctor!'

'All right, Bren.' Melvyn patted his wife's knee. 'It's probably nothing. It's not the first time I've caught a ball in the eye.'

'It's the first time it's been this bad,' she retorted.

'From the amount of bruising, that looks as if it hurts,' Holly said. 'Are you taking any painkillers, Melvyn?'

'Ibuprofen. But they're not doing much,' he admitted.

'You might be lucky and just have a bit of bruising and swelling. Though if the ball was travelling hard enough you might have fractured the bone around your eye socket—what we call an orbital blow-out. What happens is that the ball pushes your eye in, and the pressure makes the weakest bit of the bone give way—that's the bottom bit in the socket. If you want to blind everyone at work with the medical details, it's the posteromedial floor.'

'Does that mean he'll need surgery?' Brenda Platt asked.

'Depends.' Holly smiled at her. 'I need to examine your husband's eye properly before I can give you a proper diagnosis. Would you prefer to wait outside, or would you like to stay?'

'Can I stay, please?' Brenda's voice held a sharp note of anxiety.

'Of course you can.'

'Just don't interrupt the doc, love,' Melvyn said.

'I'm worried. You could go blind.'

'We'll do our best, Mrs Platt. Right, Melvyn, can you look up for me?'

'I'm trying. But it hurts.'

'How about from side to side?'

He definitely had limited movement in his bruised left eye. 'OK, you can stop now.' She smiled at him. 'You said you had double vision. Is that since the accident, or did you have any problems before?'

'Just since,' he said.

'Has it changed at all—got worse or better?'

He shrugged. 'It's hard to tell. But it'll go. These things always do.'

'Maybe, but it's also a very good idea to check them out rather than leave them. Can you read these letters for me, please?' She pointed to the Snellen chart on the wall. 'We'll do your good eye first. From the top, whenever you're ready.'

Melvyn coped fine with his right eye. But with his left, the vision was poor. Holly recorded the figures on his chart, then checked his pupils and response to light and recorded them. 'I'm going to send you for a CT scan—that's a special type of X-ray, done with a computer, which shows much more detailed images of your body in little slices,' she said. 'I have a feeling that you do have an orbital fracture, and one of the muscles in your eye might be trapped in the fracture, so I'm also going to refer you to an eye specialist.'

'So I'm going to need surgery?'

'The eye specialist will be able to tell you more. He'll check the pressure inside your eye—the equipment in the ophthalmology department is more accurate than the kit we use here. If you do need surgery, the specialist will probably wait for a couple more days until the swelling in your tissues has gone down, and give you some antibiotics in the meantime to make sure you don't get any infection. Cold compresses will help, too, both with the pain and with the swelling. The double vision should go in another couple of days. But, however the specialist decides to treat you, there are two really, really important things to remember as of right now. Limit your physical activity—so no more squash, no running, no going to the gym—and do *not* blow your nose for at least the next six weeks.'

'Why?' Brenda asked.

Holly squeezed her hand. She'd already pegged Brenda as a panicker, so it would frighten the poor woman even more if she heard that the contents of Melvyn's eye socket could prolapse into his maxillary sinus. 'The pressure of blowing his nose could cause more damage,' Holly said simply. 'I can prescribe some nasal drops if he needs it. If you'd like to wait here, I'll ring the specialist and get the scan sorted out.'

She returned a few minutes later. 'If you can take this form with you to the X-ray department—you turn left out of the emergency department reception and follow the corridor to the end—they'll see you as soon as possible. The eye specialist will come and see you there. Oh, and, Melvyn?'

'Yes?'

'It might be a good idea to wear safety glasses in future when you're playing racquet sports. I know they're a nuisance, but they can save you going through this again.'

'Can't you ask him just to stop playing squash, Doctor?' Brenda asked.

'I could. But then he'd get under your feet at home and drive you bananas. Buy him some safety glasses and threaten to dye his squash gear pink if he doesn't wear them,' Holly advised with a wink. 'And get his squash partner's wife to threaten the same thing, to make sure he really does wear them.'

'I'm sorry.' Her face was almost grey with anxiety. 'You must think I'm a right old fusspot.'

'Of course not. You're just worried about the man you love. And you were absolutely right to make him come in,' Holly said.

The rest of the morning passed in a blur. Holly was just about to collect her handbag and go to lunch when David walked into the rest room. 'Hi.'

'Hi.'

'Have lunch with me?'

She shook her head. 'Can't.'

'In case people talk?'

'No. I'm already booked.' The expression on his face told her he was desperate to know who she was seeing, but he was also trying not to look jealous. She decided to put him out of his misery. 'I'm seeing Jude and Zo.'

'Lunch tomorrow, then?'

'Maybe.'

'You're a hard woman to pin down. OK. How about dinner after work tomorrow? Do you like Thai food?'

'OK.' Was he going to snatch a kiss? He stood there, looking awkward. As if he wanted to, but wasn't sure if it would push her away. She smiled, stood on tiptoe and kissed the dimple in his chin. At the stunned expression on his face, she winked and headed for the canteen.

Judith and Zoe were already there. She caught their eyes, mouthed, 'Coffee?' and at their nods bought three espressos.

'I got you a chicken salad wrap,' Jude said when Holly joined them at the table. 'I was going to buy nachos, but Zo reckoned you'd give us one of your lectures about saturated fat.'

'Too true. The guacamole's fine, because of the monounsaturates in avocados—and the vitamin E—but all that fried stuff isn't good for you, *amigo*. Even though I know you could live on lard, Jude, and still look like a supermodel.' Holly grinned. 'Thanks. This is perfect.'

'You're chirpy today, Holls. Good morning?' Zoe asked.

'Yep. I had an interesting ophthalmology case.'

'Anything else?' Judith asked brightly.

Holly gave her a suspicious look. She and David had been careful. Or had they been spotted in the café on Sunday morning? 'No. Why?'

'Oh, nothing. Hey, you missed a brilliant film on Sunday night.'

'Jude, darling, what you call a brilliant film isn't necessarily the same as my definition,' Holly said with a grin.

'Oh, you two.' Zoe rolled her eyes. 'So—are we doing Giovanni's tomorrow night?'

'Sorry, I'm on a late. You'll have to annex your husbands to get your pizza fix,' Holly said.

'Holl, you're on an early today. Which means you're on an early tomorrow and a late on Saturday,' Judith said.

Damn. She'd forgotten how easy it was to work out her off-duty hours. 'I can't make it—I'll join you next week,' Holly said quickly, hoping that Zoe would change the topic.

No chance. Zoe pounced. 'Why can't you make it?'

'I'm going out.'

'Departmental meal?' Zoe asked.

If she said yes...Judith and Zoe knew her so well, they'd just know she was fibbing. Plus, it would be easy for them to check up—and she'd already lied to them about it and been caught out. She sighed. 'No.'

'Date?' Judith asked, raising an eyebrow.

'Mmm,' Holly muttered, squirming. Damn. She wished she hadn't teased the pair of them quite so much on their hen nights. What was that saying? *What goes around comes around.* So she was in for a severe amount of teasing now.

'Holls, this is the first time you've dated since...' Judith shook her head. 'Since I can't remember.'

Holly pulled a face. 'Listen, just because you two are old and married— What?' she demanded, seeing them both laughing hysterically.

'Holls, you're older than we are,' Zoe pointed out.

'OK. You're *young* and married, then. Just because I'm going on a date, it doesn't follow that I'm looking for love's great dream.'

'What's his name?' Zoe asked.

Holly sighed. 'I'm trying to keep it quiet. Very quiet. His name's David.'

'David Neave,' Zoe whispered back.

Holly's jaw dropped. 'The grapevine's *that* fast?'

'No...but you live next door to my sister-in-law,' Judith reminded her. When she'd married Kieran she'd moved into his house, and Tess and Charlie had moved into

Judith's old place, next door to Holly. 'She spotted a man bearing bright orange gerberas on Sunday evening. Which are now sitting on your kitchen window-sill. Which happens to face hers. She also described the man to me. And I met him this morning when he referred a case up to us.'

'Give me strength.' Holly rolled her eyes. 'So you were just waiting for me to confess?'

'Of course we weren't,' Zoe said. 'And, before you start panicking, we're the only ones who know. We've sworn Brad and Kieran to secrecy.'

'On pain of no sex ever, ever again, if they allow a single word to escape,' Judith added.

Holly held up her hands in surrender, laughing. 'You two are impossible.'

'Holls, we just want to see you happy. If he's Dr Right, we've already chosen our bridesmaids' dresses. And if he's not—well, we're here when you need to talk,' Zoe said simply.

'It's early days,' Holly warned. 'We're taking it slowly.'

Judith and Zoe exchanged a significant look, and Holly groaned inwardly. They already had her married to the man. And if she told them about the past and the truth about her gap year—that it had been in the middle of her A levels, not after it… Maybe later. Definitely *not* yet.

CHAPTER SIX

THE following Wednesday evening, Holly pressed the intercom outside David's flat and he buzzed her up.

'I think I should have worn my dark glasses,' Holly said as she walked in. The décor—which she really, really hoped wasn't his taste—was retro 1970s. Loud. Brash. And utterly unsuited to his tiny flat.

Her thoughts must have been written all over her face, because he gave her a shamefaced grin. 'OK, so it's not the kind of thing you want to face after a night shift. My landlord has rather definite ideas. I haven't sold my place in Newcastle yet, so I'm renting until that's sorted out.'

So it wasn't his taste. Good. 'It'll keep me awake at least,' she said, returning the grin and handing him a carrier bag. 'For you. Seeing as you're cooking dinner for me.'

He looked in the bag. 'New Zealand sauvignon blanc. Very nice.'

'Ahem.' She nodded to the bag. 'There's something else in there.'

He rummaged in the bag, fished out the box and inspected the contents. 'Chocolate?'

'Better than chocolate.'

'Better than sex?'

There was a long, long silence. With an expression of utter horror on his face, David muttered, 'Sorry. I didn't actually mean to say that.'

She raised an eyebrow. 'Just as well we're keeping this quiet, or it'd be going straight in the department's "quotes of note" book.'

'Come and sit down.' He ushered her into the kitchen-diner and seated her so that her back was to the kitchen area.

The first course—spoonfuls of smoked salmon pâté wrapped in smoked salmon and tied with a chive—was glorious. She couldn't believe David had been able to see straight enough to tie the chive, considering how fiddly it was and how little sleep he must have had following the night shift. But she was touched that he'd made the effort.

It was followed by chicken in white wine and tarragon sauce, with baby new potatoes and baby vegetables. Again, it was beautifully presented. She'd had no idea that he could cook this well…or could he?

Her suspicions were confirmed when he produced two glasses filled with home-made white chocolate mousse. She recognised the glasses—she had a few of them herself. And she knew exactly which aisle and even which shelf to look at in the supermarket's chiller cabinet to find them.

'Gorgeous. This must have taken you ages. You must give me the recipe.'

He mumbled something she didn't catch.

A confession, or not?

She decided to give him the benefit of the doubt. 'Have you tried the lemon mousse in this range? It's pretty good.'

He winced. 'I was really hoping you weren't going to recognise them.'

'They're Jude's favourite. I've eaten them enough times—of course I recognised them.' She gave him a side-long look. 'So when were you going to confess properly?'

'Later. Actually, I did cook something myself. But I was so nervous that I burned it and I had to rush out to get this.'

Holly stared at him in surprise. 'We could have got a take-away. Am I really that scary?'

'Yes. No.' David raked a hand through his hair. 'I just wanted it to be perfect. But my flat's horrible and the food was rubbish and—'

'Hey. I've come to see you, not your flat.'

'Yeah.' He smiled ruefully. 'We need your better-than-chocolate gianduja stuff, I think.'

'No.' She came to stand behind him, put her arms around him and rested her cheek against his. 'You've made a fuss of me, and I appreciate it. I'm sorry for teasing.'

A beat passed. 'How sorry?' he asked, his voice low and husky.

'This sorry.' She kissed his cheek.

'Not enough.'

'This sorry.' She kissed the hollow behind his ear.

'Still not enough.'

She rubbed her cheek against his and whispered, 'Tough. That's all you get, because you're facing the wrong way.'

She wasn't sure how it happened, but the next thing she knew she was sitting on his lap and David was kissing her. Very thoroughly.

When he finally let her come up for breath, she rested her forehead against his. 'I thought we were supposed to be taking things slowly?'

'We are. You had dinner with me on Friday night.' At the Thai restaurant, after their late shift. Then he'd walked her home, stayed for just long enough to kiss her goodnight and left her wanting more. A lot more. 'We haven't seen each other outside work since then.'

Until tonight. When he'd suggested cooking dinner for them.

And now she was sitting on his lap. Nearly as close as they could get with their clothes on. 'This doesn't feel like slow to me.' She wriggled slightly closer. 'How's your self-control?'

He swallowed hard. 'Splintering. How's yours?'

'Pretty much the same.' They'd agreed to take it slowly this time. But she didn't want to any more. Not when he had that look on his face. The look that reminded her of the very first time they'd made love.

Thirteen years ago.

There was slow, and there was *slow*. She wanted him. Needed him. 'What colour's your bedroom?'

He groaned. 'It's purple. *Dark* purple. You'll hate it.'

'Maybe you should get your landlord to give you a rent rebate, on the grounds of using dangerous colours.' She grinned. 'Lighten up.'

'That's my line.'

'I borrowed it.' Her eyes met his. 'So what are we going to do?'

'About what?'

'You and me.' She tilted her pelvis, enough to make him gasp. 'This.'

'I wanted our first time—this time round—to be different. Candlelight, champagne, red roses…the lot.' His eyes were all soft and dreamy. 'You, me, a country hotel and an antique four-poster.'

'With an antique lumpy mattress?'

'No. With a nice new mattress.' He ran his tongue over his lower lip and it was all she could do not to rip his clothes off. 'Because I don't want anything taking your attention off what I'm going to do to you.'

Promises, promises. And they were written very clearly in his eyes. Desire shimmered through her.

'So when precisely did you think about doing this?'

'We're both off duty tomorrow.'

'Slow's off, then?'

His eyes narrowed slightly, and then he sighed. 'OK. I'll wait until you're ready. Your terms.'

Holly wriggled a tiny bit closer and rocked against him. Colour flared in his cheeks and his pupils darkened. So he was just as hot and bothered about this as she was… 'Tomorrow sounds good to me,' she whispered.

His breathing quickened. 'Are you sure about this, Hol?'

'Absolutely.' So sure, she'd be quite happy to take her chances with a horrible dark purple bedroom.

So what if they'd only worked together for two weeks? They'd actually met fourteen years ago. They'd been together for two years. And the twelve years in between suddenly didn't matter any more.

'You'll spend your day off with me tomorrow?'

'Yep.'

'Then I'll pick you up in the morning. Half past nine, so the rush-hour's out of the way.'

'Where are we going?'

'Nice hotel. Countryside. I dunno. Somewhere. Anywhere.' He shook his head. 'We don't have to get back for work on Friday morning. Unless you'd rather wait a while?'

'Would you?' she asked, knowing that she didn't want to wait.

'No.' He slid his hands into her hair, drew her face back to his and kissed her. Tiny butterfly kisses along her lower lip, until her mouth was tingling. And then a full-on kiss, his tongue stroking along hers, until she was shivering all over and desperate to remove the last barriers between them.

'I think, Holly Jones, I'd better take you home. Now. Before my self-control goes completely.'

'What if I don't want to go home?' she asked huskily.

'Tough. Because when I rediscover all the places you like to be touched, all the places you like to be kissed, I

don't want it to be here.' He held her gaze. 'I want it to
be perfect, Hol.'

'Nothing's perfect, David.'

He smiled. 'Tell me that on Friday morning.'

Despite the fact that she was tired, Holly hardly slept that
night. Wanting David. Wondering whether she was doing
the right thing. Whether they'd both gone completely crazy.
OK, so she'd loved him desperately first time round. But
they weren't eighteen any more. They'd grown up,
changed. He was divorced. She was dedicated to her career.

It wasn't too late to stop this. They'd spent a couple of
evenings together, shared a few kisses. They hadn't made
a commitment to each other. She could just ring him tomorrow and tell him that she'd changed her mind.

The problem was, she didn't want to.

And she had a nasty suspicion that there was a much,
much bigger problem. Like the fact that she might—just
might—never have fallen out of love with David Neave.
Which meant that if he broke her heart again, this time it
would be for keeps.

At twenty-five past nine the next morning, Holly's doorbell
buzzed.

'It's not too late to change your mind,' David said softly
when she opened the door.

'Is it that obvious?' She closed the door behind him.

'You look…nervous.'

She lifted her chin. 'Of course I'm not.'

He brushed the back of his fingers against her cheek. 'I
am.'

She blinked. '*You're* nervous?'

'Mmm-hmm.'

She raised an eyebrow. 'And this is the man who promised me perfection.'

'Bravado. Bluff. Bluster.' His smile didn't quite reach his eyes. 'Supposing I don't live up to my promise?'

Somehow, she thought he would. When their bodies finally fused again, it would be like nothing else on earth. She wouldn't be able to think or breathe anything else except him. 'How about we do this with no expectations? No promises. Just see where this leads us. Like we agreed.'

'I know what I want to do,' he said, very softly. 'I want to carry you back upstairs to bed right now. Sleep with you in my arms. And then, when we wake, I want to explore you. All over. With my hands, my mouth. Until I know who you really are—Scary Holly or Nice Holly.'

If he kept saying things like this, her knees definitely weren't going to work. 'Maybe I'm both.'

'Maybe. I want to kiss you, Hol—but if I do, I won't be able to stop, and I had other plans for today.'

'Such as?'

He grinned. 'Wait and see. Your chariot awaits.'

The chariot turned out to be an elderly sports car.

'It's mechanically sound,' David assured her.

'Right. And what about the rust spots?'

'I haven't quite finished restoring it.'

'So this is what you spend your time off doing?' He hadn't been a car nut years ago. He'd learned to drive, just as she had, but he hadn't been one of the guys who'd spent all his spare time with his nose under the bonnet of a car or in a car magazine, drooling over pictures of vintage prestige marquees and planning how they were going to spend their entire salaries on a piece of machinery when they started work.

'When I was in Newcastle, yes. This was a wreck. I got

help with the engine, and I've been working on the body ever since.'

'Right.'

'It's perfectly safe. It's roadworthy, Hol, or I wouldn't have been able to get road tax for it.'

'I suppose.'

He put her bags in the boot while she climbed into the passenger side. Old-fashioned seat belts, too—and the last person who'd sat here had been a lot bigger than she was. She adjusted the belt and clicked it in place.

David joined her and she nodded at the CD player. 'Is this meant to be an authentic restoration?'

He wrinkled his nose. 'Nearly. I couldn't drive without music.'

It wasn't so surprising. He was the only person she'd ever known who'd had a bigger music collection than hers. She flicked through the CDs. 'Your taste hasn't changed, then.'

'It's broadened a bit. Anything there you'd like to hear?'

'Hmm.' She picked an old favourite and slid it into the CD player. Half an hour later, they were out of London and Holly found she was enjoying herself. Driving fast, in a classic car, with music she loved playing slightly too loud.

Just as she'd imagined things would be, when they were teenagers.

Her smile faded. So much for forgetting the past. How could she when it was still so very much *there*?

She'd expected him to drive to a hotel. Instead, he turned into the entrance of a zoo.

'It's years since I've been to a zoo,' Holly said.

'You took me to see the sharks, so I'm taking you to see the lions. Don't scare them, OK?'

'Oh, very funny.' But his smile was infectious.

'The zoo's got a good reputation—the habitat's as natural as possible and they make the animals work for their food, so they don't get bored. You won't see animals pacing up and down cages here.'

'I would've brought my camera if I'd known we were seeing lions,' she said as they walked to the turnstiles.

'And snow leopards. My favourites,' David said. 'But, seeing as you mentioned it…' He took a tiny silver-coloured box from his pocket.

'*That's* a camera?'

'Digital,' he explained.

She rolled her eyes. 'Boys and their toys.'

He slid an arm around her shoulders. 'Says the woman who has her own treadmill. And a state-of-the-art sound system.'

She leaned into him, laughing. 'It's a fair cop. I admit I'm a gadget freak, too.' Something else they had in common.

They wandered round the zoo together. And when they got to the lions, David persuaded another visitor to take a photograph of them together with the lions in the background.

It was the kind of thing they would have done—*had* done—as teenagers. Her stomach knotted. Was it all going to go wrong again?

Her fears must have shown on her face because David held her closer. She heard him take a breath, as if he was about to say something, and then they both heard the screams.

They ran towards the sound. A woman was screaming, a toddler was sobbing and a man with a red face looked as if he was trying to calm them both down.

'That—that *thing* bit my baby!' the woman sobbed. 'It

should be put down! They shouldn't have dangerous animals like that around here!'

Holly and David exchanged a glance.

'We're doctors,' David said gently. 'Can we help?'

'It's just a graze—all it needs is a plaster,' the man said. 'She's crying from shock more than anything else.'

'What happened?'

'The monkey just *flew* at our daughter and bit her!' The woman was still shaking.

'Let me have a look,' Holly offered. 'Hey, can you be a brave girl and let me look at where it hurts?'

'No. Bitey!' the little girl sobbed.

'What's her name?' Holly asked the mother.

'Cara.'

'Cara, I'm going to tell you a secret—something I don't tell everyone,' Holly said. 'I'm a fairy princess. So I can sprinkle some magic dust on your hand to make it stop hurting.'

The little girl gave her a suspicious look, as if to say that fairy princesses had long blonde hair, not short dark hair, but then she held her hand out. Holly made a great show of sprinkling magic fairy dust, explaining that it was so magic that humans couldn't even see it, and Cara calmed down enough to let Holly examine the bite.

'What happened?' David asked the father.

'I dunno. I put Cara on my shoulders so she could see the monkeys. She must have leaned forward and grabbed the bars or something—at the top, where there isn't the extra wire. The next thing I knew, the monkey charged against the bars and she started screaming and her hand was bleeding.'

'It's your fault. You went too close. And my baby...' The woman started sobbing again.

'It's not very deep,' Holly said.

'I told you, love,' the man said to his wife. 'It just needs a plaster.'

'Actually, no,' Holly said. 'You need to get it washed out properly, with salt water. And I'd pop along to the local casualty department and get them to check it over.'

The woman stopped crying and stared in shock. 'Casualty? It's that serious?'

'All bites need to be checked by a doctor, even if they don't look very deep,' Holly said. Bites to the hand could be serious—they sometimes caused nerve damage. 'Even your average moggy can pass on something pretty nasty—their mouths often contain bacteria such as streptococcus or fusibacteria, which can make the wound turn septic.'

'And it's worse with wild animals?' the man asked.

Holly and David exchanged a glance. He gave the slightest shake of his head, signifying that he didn't think the mother would be able to cope with the idea that monkey bites could cause the herpes simplex infection—a virus which could cause nasty blisters—and the toddler might be given aciclovir, an antiviral drug, to help prevent the infection.

'I'd need to check with an infections specialist,' Holly said. 'I'm more used to dealing with bites from cats, dogs and humans in the emergency department. What I can say is that I usually give antibiotics to stop any nasty infections developing.'

'If I were you,' David added, 'I'd get your little one to the first-aid people here, ask them to wash the graze thoroughly but don't put a plaster on, then just pop in to Casualty and ask them to take a look.'

'My chocolate,' Cara wailed.

'Was she eating chocolate when you put her on your shoulders?' Holly asked.

The father grimaced. 'Yes.'

'I think that's what the monkey must have been after, not her fingers,' David said.

'Would you like us to come with you to First Aid?' Holly asked.

'Would you?' The man gave her a grateful look.

'Sure.'

After they'd talked to the first-aid people, then given a report to the zoo's admin about the accident, David and Holly had a lazy lunch on the café terrace, then wandered around the rest of the zoo, their arms wrapped around each other.

'It's been fun,' Holly said.

'Yeah. Though I get the feeling that Cara isn't going to sit on her dad's shoulders for a long, long time,' David said wryly. 'You're very good with children.'

'Mmm.' Holly couldn't help thinking of their own child. The baby she'd lost. The children they'd planned to have.

'Hey. We're supposed to be ignoring the past,' he reminded her.

She smiled wryly. So he could still read her mind. 'I know. It's hard.'

'You know what you need? A whirlpool bath.'

'In a zoo?'

He chuckled. 'In our hotel. Our bathroom, to be precise.'

'You've booked us a room with a whirlpool bath? Now *that's* decadent.'

'With champagne. And strawberries. And we must have walked a fair way around this zoo…'

'Anyone would think, David Neave, that you were trying to talk me into taking my clothes off.'

His pupils darkened. 'And anyone, Holly Jones, would be absolutely right.'

She lifted one shoulder. 'Then what are we waiting for?'

CHAPTER SEVEN

THE hotel was chocolate-box pretty, half-timbered, with a thatched roof and diamond-paned windows. Inside, it was even more to Holly's liking—pale walls, dark beams and deep, deep pile carpets. It made her want to kick her shoes off and walk barefoot.

David signed them in, got the card key and carried their bags to their room.

Holly blinked as she saw the tray containing an ice bucket, champagne and a dish of strawberries sitting on the dressing table next to the four-poster bed. 'Wow. You really meant it about the champagne and strawberries.'

'And it's a new mattress. I asked.'

She laughed and sat on the bed. 'I'm not that much of a princess really.'

'It's important to have the right mattress.' He gave her a sidelong look. 'The right bed.'

A shiver ran through her. They'd made love many, many times before. But it had been years ago. This time round, would it be familiar…or would it be strange? The weirdest thing was, she felt shy.

Shy in a way she hadn't felt the very first time they'd made love.

Crazy. She was older. Wiser. She'd made love with other men since David. Not many, but enough to be sure of herself. So why was she feeling like this? So scared, so uncertain?

It must have shown in her face, her eyes, because he took her hand. 'Hol. There's no pressure. If you want to keep things as they are, that's fine. I'll stay in another room.'

'No. It's not that. It's just…' How could she explain?

'I know.' He rubbed his thumb comfortingly over the back of her hand. 'Me, too. I'll, um, sort out the whirlpool bath, shall I?'

She should have bought a black silk negligee. Something sexy. Instead, she'd packed an ordinary dressing-gown. Serviceable navy cotton, and boring as hell.

This wasn't going to work, she thought as she stripped swiftly and wrapped the dressing-gown around her. She was going to disappoint him. Maybe they should have left the past where it was.

'Bathroom's all yours,' David said, walking over to her.

At least he wasn't going to watch her take off her dressing-gown. And the whirlpool bath was warm. Deep enough to cover her embarrassment. Maybe the bubbles would start to have an effect and relax her before he joined her. She hoped.

David rapped on the door. 'Can I come in?'

'Uh—yes.'

He wore only a towel wrapped around his hips, and he was carrying a tray with two glasses of champagne and a dish of strawberries. 'Close your eyes.'

She blinked. 'What?'

'Close your eyes,' he repeated.

She did so.

'You can open them again now.'

He was sitting in the whirlpool bath next to her.

Naked, beneath the bubbles.

Her hand was shaking slightly as she accepted the glass he offered her.

'To you and me. To here and now,' he said softly, raising his own glass.

She echoed his toast, took a sip of champagne and nearly choked on the bubbles. David took the glass from her and patted her back. 'OK?' he asked, sounding worried.

She nodded. 'Just went down the wrong way.'

'Holly…' Somehow they were facing each other and his hand slid down her back, smoothing the curve of her spine. Skin to skin. And it wasn't anywhere near enough. She arched against him and slid her fingers into his hair. And then he was kissing her, the strawberries and the champagne forgotten. He cupped her breasts, his thumbs brushing against her hardening nipples, and she shuddered with need.

'Hol.' He bent his head and kissed the hollows of her collar-bone. She urged him on, tightening her fingers against his scalp. He teased her, following the line of her collar-bone to the other shoulder. And then, at last, he drew one nipple into his mouth.

She closed her eyes in bliss. This was good. Better than good. But it still wasn't enough. She wanted him. All of him. Now.

As if he'd read her mind, he pulled her onto his lap so she was sitting astride him. 'Hol. I need you.'

'Now,' she murmured, lifting herself slightly.

When he entered her, it felt like coming home. As if he'd been away for a long, long time in a lonely, dangerous world and at last he was back. Safe. Where he'd craved to be.

This wasn't just sex. This was *Holly*. Holly, the woman he'd never been able to forget. Then, she'd been a shy, bookish teenager. Now, she was a woman. Still shy with him at first, but now she was moving over him. Teasing him, rubbing the tips of her breasts against his chest.

Squeezing her internal muscles around him, pushing his desire to a higher pitch.

And he loved every second of it.

More than that.

He loved *her*.

He couldn't possibly tell her. It was way, way too soon. Too many fences still needed to be mended. If he took it too fast now, the whole lot could collapse again. But this— this was the beginning of the rest of his life. And he was happier than he could remember being in years.

'You're beautiful,' he murmured in her ear. 'All woman.'

And all *mine*.

Not that he was stupid enough to voice that one. This was Scary Holly, the woman who'd had to treat the mugger who'd attacked her. But she was also Sexy Holly, the woman who was making love with him in a whirlpool bath, responding to the way he touched her. He loved everything about this. Her scent. The way she tasted. The weight of her breasts in his hands. The softness of her skin. The way her breathing had changed, becoming faster and more shallow as her arousal grew.

And then she was rippling round him and his body was surging against hers. She cried out his name and he muffled it with his mouth, kissing her hungrily, wanting everything she could give and then some.

When he came down from the peak, she was still straddling him, wrapped in his arms, with her head on his shoulder. He knew Holly could fight her own battles—this was the woman who could quiet the rowdiest drunks on a Saturday night in the emergency department—but right here, right now, he wanted to protect her. Be her knight in shining armour. Be everything he hadn't been last time in her eyes. He kissed the curve of her neck.

'Hol, there's a limit on how long we're supposed to spend in a whirlpool bath.'

'Don't ask me when we passed it.' Her voice was soft, almost slurred. 'You know what? I don't even care.'

'If we don't get out of here, we're going to look like prunes.'

'So?'

'So we're supposed to be having dinner.' Gently, he lifted her off him. Soaped her all over. Rinsed her. Then lifted her out of the whirlpool bath and wrapped her in a huge fluffy towel.

'Not fair.' She gave him an exaggerated pout as he slid back into the tub to wash. 'Don't I get to do the same for you?'

The look in her eyes nearly made him drag her back in the whirlpool bath with him, towel and all. But he wanted to romance her tonight. Have dinner with her. Talk to her. Maybe dance with her. Hold her close. And then make love with her again. 'Dinner first,' he said huskily. 'If you put one finger on me, you won't be seeing anything but this bathroom for a week.'

'No can do. We're back at work on Sunday morning. Early shift.' She blew him a kiss, sashayed over to the door—and dropped her towel. Before he could act on his instincts and climb out of the tub to grab her, she turned her head, winked at him and closed the bathroom door.

David needed a cold shower. A long, cold shower—and even that didn't work too well, because he nearly cut himself shaving when he started thinking about Holly and shivered with desire.

He wrapped a towel around his hips and returned to the bedroom.

Holly raised an eyebrow. 'I thought women were supposed to be the ones who spent ages in the bathroom?'

'Ha.' He eyed her dressing-gown. 'I thought you'd be dressed.'

'Give me five minutes.' She took a pile of things from the bed, walked into the bathroom and shut the door behind her.

Definitely not an invitation to join her, then.

Which was probably a good thing. Otherwise they wouldn't make dinner.

He was dressed when she opened the door again. And his jaw dropped when he saw her. She was wearing a very simple shift dress and the minimum of make-up. But she looked absolutely stunning, from the tips of her high-heeled red shoes to the neat gamin haircut he wanted to disorder. Right now. Along with kissing every scrap of lipstick off her mouth.

This wasn't the awkward teenager he remembered. This wasn't Dr Jones, the efficient emergency specialist who never, but never, wore a skirt at work. The woman in front of him was a sex goddess in red silk. Every man's dream woman.

She wiggled her hips at him. 'Do I pass muster?'

'Oh, yes.' Hell. His voice had even dropped an octave or so. How was he going to be able to walk out of this room, when all he wanted to do was rip those clothes off her again and spread her underneath him on the bed?

She ran her thumb along his lower lip. 'You're drooling.'

'Am not.' Was he?

She grinned. 'Gotcha.'

He pulled her close, making sure she knew exactly how aroused he was. Like from nought to a hundred in one second flat. 'I've changed my mind. You're not scary, Holly Jones, you're dangerous.'

So was he, Holly thought. She'd never seen David in a suit—well, apart from when they'd gone for their university interviews. But he'd been little more than a boy then. A gawky teenager, dressed in a suit that hadn't really fitted him properly. Whereas this…this wasn't off the peg. His suit was definitely made to measure. Good-quality material. Probably his ex-wife's influence. She was something in the media, so she knew the importance of appearances.

Holly ignored the stab of jealousy. The past was the past. She couldn't change it. Whereas the future started here.

'Shall we go?' she asked.

David slid the room's card key into his pocket, tucked her arm into his and escorted her down to the dining room. 'Your legs are incredible. I can't ever remember seeing you wear a dress,' he said. 'Or high heels.'

'I don't very often.'

'Just as well. If you walked down the high street in that, there'd be a line of suspected MIs in the department within seconds.'

She grinned. 'My dress isn't *that* short.'

'Maybe. But I happen to know what's underneath it, and that's enough to give me an MI,' he murmured, and she felt colour flood into her cheeks.

'Behave,' she muttered.

But when they were seated in the dining room, studying the menu, she noticed him frowning.

'What's up?' she asked.

'I can't choose.'

'Too much choice?'

He shook his head. 'Just…not hungry.'

'Neither am I.' Not for food, anyway. She slipped one foot out of her shoe and caressed his ankle with her toes.

He swallowed hard. 'Are you saying what I think you're saying?'

She nodded, not trusting her voice.

'Let's get room service,' David whispered.

No way were they going to be able to have breakfast in the dining room tomorrow morning. She was sure that all the other diners were staring at them as they walked out again. Knowing why they were leaving. Reading their minds.

But David was holding her hand. Very tightly. So she didn't really care what other people thought. All that mattered was being with him, skin to skin. Touching. Tasting. Rediscovering.

The second the door closed behind them she took off his jacket. It hit the floor, but they'd both gone past caring about crumpled fabric. His tie was next—silk, she noticed. As smooth as his freshly shaven skin. And then, one by one, she undid the buttons of his shirt.

Desire kicked in her stomach. There was something incredibly arousing about a man in formal dress, slightly *déshabillé*. Especially one built like David. She couldn't resist running her hands over his chest, feeling the hardness of his muscles under the silky-soft sprinkling of hair. He was definitely broader than she remembered. Stronger. And very, very masculine.

He caught her hands as they splayed over his washboard-flat stomach, drew them to his mouth and kissed them. 'My turn now,' he whispered.

He unzipped her dress and let the silk pool around her feet, then took a step back. 'Wow,' he said, his voice low and husky. 'Do you have any idea how incredible you look, how long your legs are in those shoes? Uh, and stockings. If I'd had the least idea, I don't think I could've let you leave this room in the first place.'

She took a step forward and he dropped to his knees. He nuzzled her stomach, and then she felt his tongue circling her navel. She arched against him, wanting more, and he took advantage of her position to unsnap the clasp of her bra.

His pupils darkened as he looked up, and colour bloomed on his cheekbones. 'What a view,' he murmured, straightening up and touching the tip of his tongue to the hard peak of her nipple. 'Hol, you're so beautiful.'

She moved instinctively towards him and slid her fingers into his hair, wanting him to take her into his mouth, and almost sagged in disappointment when he pulled away.

'Not yet,' he said softly. 'I haven't finished exploring.'

She shivered as she felt his thumbs skimming along her inner thighs, and then he rolled one hold-up stocking down her leg. He stroked her thigh, her calf, her ankle, then slid her foot out of her shoe and slowly finished removing the stocking, rubbing the arch of her foot as he did so. The other stocking followed suit, and Holly was quivering by the time he'd finished. Needing. Wanting. Why was he making her wait?

'Not yet,' he whispered against her thigh. The teasing movement of his mouth against her skin—so near, but not near enough—drove her crazy.

'Please,' she begged, but he had his own agenda.

Slowly, so slowly that she thought she was going to go insane, he worked his way down her leg, kissing the back of her knee, the hollow of her ankle. 'Your nail varnish matches your knickers,' he murmured, caressing her foot and kissing each toe in turn. 'You always were fussy about details.'

Fussy? She was going to combust if he didn't take her to bed right now.

And then he started again on her other foot, slowly moving upwards. Holly tilted her pelvis, wanting him to shed the last barrier between them—wanting him to rip her knickers off and soothe the raging heat between her thighs.

'Please. Now,' she begged.

'This time's meant to be slow and easy,' he murmured against her inner thigh.

She couldn't wait for slow and easy. 'I want hard and fast.'

'No, you don't. Trust me.' And then he went even slower, until Holly thought he'd drive her completely out of her mind. He explored every inch of her skin with his hands and his mouth, making her desire burn hotter and hotter. Holly was at the point of hyperventilating when he picked her up and laid her against the cool cotton sheets on the four-poster.

At last. At last. She reached out to take the rest of his clothes off, but he stilled her hands. 'Shh. Not yet. There's something I need first.' He slid one finger underneath the hem of her red silk knickers. Holly pushed towards him, wanting him, and then at last he was touching her properly.

As his clever fingers moved, he was watching her intently. Watching her eyes. As he brought her to the peak, he watched her dissolve—and smiled as she cried out his name.

'That's what I wanted. Needed. To know you were seeing me,' he said softly.

'I was seeing you,' she said. 'Uh. I feel as if I've run a marathon. Slow, but not easy.'

'It's better if you wait.'

'Really? Like to prove that, would you?'

'Is that an offer?'

'Oh, yes.' And she was going to tease him just as much as he'd teased her.

Starting with removing his clothes.

His shirt first. Holly spent a lot of time exploring the muscles of his chest and coaxing his flat nipples into hardness. She traced the dark arrowing of hair down to his navel, and smiled when he reacted instinctively by tilting his pelvis. 'Slow and easy, you said,' she reminded him.

His socks came off next. He had nice feet—and the soft skin on his soles used to be ticklish. A brief experiment told her that it still was.

Next, his trousers. She took a long time undoing the button. And even longer undoing the zip. She could feel how ready he was for her; she caught his gaze and moistened her lower lip deliberately, making him groan. She blew him a kiss, then commanded softly, 'Lift your hips for me.' He did, and she slowly worked the fabric down over his buttocks, pausing to caress his thighs and calves as she removed his trousers.

By the time she'd removed his jockey shorts, he was definitely at the quivering stage.

So now you know what it feels like, she thought.

And now *she* knew what it felt like on the other side. Powerful. Heady. Knowing that he was so turned on a single touch from her could blow his mind.

'Now?' she asked.

'Almost now.' He reached over to the bedside cabinet and took a foil packet from the drawer.

'Mine, I think,' she said. She held his gaze as she opened the packet and unrolled the condom over him.

'*Now.*' His voice was so thick with desire she could barely hear him.

She straddled him. Tilted her hips to tease him for a moment. Then finally sheathed him inside her body.

'Ah, Holly.' He pulled his upper body off the bed so he could wrap his arms around her and kiss her.

Holly couldn't remember sex being this good. Ever. Even with David, the first time round, twelve years ago. She couldn't remember anyone making her feel as though he was breathing his soul into her when he kissed her.

He rolled her over onto her back, still sheathed inside her, and thrust deep.

'Yes,' she hissed, closing her eyes.

He stopped. 'No.'

'What?'

'Don't close your eyes.' He bent down to kiss her. 'I want to see you. I want you to see me. When.'

He moved again and she still wasn't quite coherent. 'When what?'

'When…' Pause. 'We…' Pause. 'Come…'

His eyes were almost midnight blue. And then the blue seemed to splinter into a thousand galaxies.

Some time later—Holly wasn't sure exactly how much time later—she lay curled in David's arms, feeling more at peace with herself and the world than she had in years.

'I was wrong,' she said softly.

'Hmm? Wrong about what?'

'When I said nothing's perfect.' Her smile felt a mile wide. 'I think that was.'

He kissed the tip of her nose. 'You're good for my ego.'

'Mmm. And you're good for certain bits of my anatomy.'

He chuckled and held her closer. 'Want to try dinner now?'

'My dress and your suit won't be fit for wearing until they've been dry-cleaned and pressed.' She smiled. 'We did have some strawberries and champagne.'

'The champagne'll be flat by now. And the strawberries will be past their best.' He rubbed his cheek against hers. 'Let's do the decadent thing. Dinner in bed. Let's order room service.'

'Sounds good.'

'Anything you'd like in particular?'

Her smile broadened. 'I don't think it's on the menu.'

He nipped gently at her earlobe. 'That can be arranged. Later…'

CHAPTER EIGHT

'Hol. Holly.' David shook her. 'Wake up. Coffee.'

'Uh.' She yawned, sat up and took the mug from him. 'Thanks. I think. What time is it?'

'Quarter to six. We have to be out of here in an hour.'

'*You* have to be out of here,' she corrected.

He frowned. 'So do you. We're on early shift, remember.'

'You are. I'm not. I switched with Trish.'

'What? Why?'

She grimaced. 'Sorry. I forgot to tell you. Trish is doing my late on Wednesday and I'm doing her late today.'

He still looked puzzled. 'What's special about Wednesday?'

'The fundraiser.' At his blank look, she said, 'If I haven't made you buy a ticket yet, I must be slipping. Zo, Jude and I do a fundraiser once a month. Zo does the food, Jude sings and I make people buy tickets. We split the proceeds between Paeds, Maternity and Emergency.' She smiled.

'Yup, you're slipping,' David told her. 'It's the first I've heard of it.'

'I've had some—' she gave him her wickedest smile '—distractions, you could say. So, are you going to buy a ticket?'

He rolled his eyes. 'OK. For you, I'll buy a ticket. Even though I won't be able to make it.'

'It doesn't start until half past eight, so you'll only miss the first half-hour or so if you come straight after your shift.'

'Fine.' He climbed back into bed beside her. 'I hate the idea of leaving you here in bed while I'm on the ward.'

'Tough.' She wrinkled her nose at him. 'I'm all nice and warm. I don't have to be on the ward for another seven hours. So I'm staying put.'

'I'm almost tempted to throw a sickie.'

Her eyes widened. 'You'll do no such thing, David Neave. Not when you're on my ward. And I don't care if you *are* my senior.'

He lifted his hands in surrender. 'OK, Dr Scary. You win.'

'I'll leave you something nice for lunch,' she promised.

'Here?'

'Ah, yes. You'll need a key.'

He went very still. 'You're giving me a key to your house?'

'It makes sense. Seeing as we've, um, spent more time here than anywhere else in the last few days.' Since their night at the little country hotel they'd spent all their off-duty time together, unable to bear being apart. David's purple bedroom had been too much for Holly to stomach, so they'd stayed at Holly's. David had only been back to his flat to grab a change of clothes and get rid of the things that had gone off in his fridge.

'Hol, am I being dense, or are you saying you want me to move in?'

She smiled at him. 'If you want to. I know we said we were going to take it slowly this time. But it's not as if we've only just met.'

'And we've wasted twelve years already.'

'So what's the point of wasting any more time—?'

'When this feels so right?' he finished.

'Exactly.'

He kissed her. 'Hol. I don't know what to say.'

'Think about it and tell me tonight. Because you, Dr Neave, are on duty very shortly.'

'Give me your keys when you come on duty,' he said. 'And I'll have dinner ready when you come home.'

Home.

Holly had adored her house since the moment she'd bought it. She'd always thought of it as home. But now she realised there had been something missing for all those years.

David.

And now…everything was perfect.

'Handover,' David said. 'Let's go to my office.'

'You call that an office?' Holly teased. 'It's the size of a broom cupboard!'

'Big enough to do a handover.' The second they were in his office, he pulled her into his arms and kissed her hard. 'Mmm. That's better.'

'We're supposed to be at work,' she reminded him.

He sighed. 'You want to keep it quiet?'

'For now.'

'OK. Work it is.' He switched into efficient doctor mode and took her through the patients who were waiting to see a specialist, the ones under observation who might need admitting and the ones that he thought they could send home that afternoon. 'That's about it.'

'Fine. Since you're off now, I've left you something in the fridge. And I know exactly how much better-than-chocolate is left,' she warned.

'I'm going to be too busy to raid your supplies,' David said. 'Cooking dinner for my woman. Plus doing a bit of packing.' He rubbed the tip of his nose against hers. 'And, since you suggested it, moving my stuff.' He nibbled her lower lip and she sighed, melting into his kiss.

'Go home,' she said when he broke the kiss. 'You're distracting me and I have patients to see.'

'That would have sounded more effective if your legs hadn't been wrapped around my waist,' he murmured into her ear.

'My legs aren't… Oh.' She flushed as she realised just where her legs were. 'When did that happen?'

He grinned. 'Hey, I'm not complaining.'

'I am. I'm on duty.' She stroked his face. 'I'll see you later.'

'Count on it.'

'Mmm, before I forget.' She took a small bunch of keys from her pocket. 'My spare set.'

'And your alarm code?'

'Zero-one-zero-four.'

'April Fool's Day?' he asked.

She chuckled. 'See. You could have guessed it all by yourself.'

'Hol. Before you go…' He pulled her back into his arms and kissed her lingeringly.

When she left his office, she really hoped she didn't look as if she'd just been thoroughly kissed. She busied herself seeing patients.

Most of the cases were routine—until she ushered Tiffany Baker into Cubicle Three.

'I'm not that ill, really. My boyfriend's making a fuss. It's just flu,' Tiffany said.

'There isn't any flu going round.'

'Jet lag, then.'

He shook his head. 'She got back from Thailand two weeks ago. And she's burning up—that's why I brought her in.'

An alarm bell rang in Holly's head. Flu-like symptoms,

a high temperature and Tiffany had been in Thailand. Malaria? 'So what are your symptoms?' she asked.

'Hot, tired and headachy.' Tiffany shrugged. 'I just need stronger headache tablets, that's all.'

'And you've just come back from Thailand?'

'Yes. I'm a magazine photographer—I did a shoot there a couple of weeks ago.'

Tiffany was shivering, Holly noticed, and sweating. It could be flu, but she had a nasty feeling it was more likely to be something more serious. 'Have you been to West Africa at all?'

'No.'

Which pretty much ruled out one of the nastiest of the nasties—Lassa fever.

'How long have you been feeling like this, Tiffany?'

'A couple of days,' her boyfriend answered. 'So I think it's more than flu.'

'Did you take anti-malaria tablets before you went?' Holly asked.

Tiffany nodded. 'Is that what you think it is?'

'Possibly. Even if you took the tablets, some of the mosquitoes around Thailand are drug-resistant. When did you take your last malaria tablet?'

'The last day I was there, which I know was too early— about two weeks ago.'

Holly checked Tiffany's temperature. Way too high. Her blood pressure was low and her heart rate was too fast: both symptoms were common with malaria. 'My gut feeling is that you've got malaria, which is a notifiable disease. It's a parasitic infection transmitted by the bite of an infected female mosquito—there are four different types, so I need to find out which it is.' If it was Plasmodium falciparum Tiffany could become very ill indeed. 'I'm going to take some blood for tests, and call in a specialist to see you.'

Tiffany's boyfriend looked slightly panicky. 'Malaria can be fatal, can't it?'

'Most of the deaths are in children under the age of five, and in developing countries,' Holly reassured him. She paused. 'Tiffany, is there any chance you could be pregnant?'

'No. We're careful, and I had my period last week.'

'I'll do a test, just to be on the safe side,' Holly said.

'So why's it taken this long for me to start feeling ill?' Tiffany asked.

'You often don't show symptoms of malaria for a couple of weeks after an infected bite—with some types it might be six weeks or longer.' Holly smiled at her. 'Basically, what's happened is that the mosquito had a quick snack out of your arm, and at the same time put the parasite in you. The parasite goes into the red blood cells and eats the haemoglobin—it scoffs sugar about seventy times as quickly as your red blood cells can metabolise it, so your blood sugar drops. Then it replicates itself inside your blood cells and puts toxic by-products into your bloodstream—that's what's causing the flu-like symptoms. It can also make you anaemic, so I'll be checking your blood count as well as doing a screen for the parasite.

'I'm going to admit you to the ward—if there aren't any complications, you'll be feeling a lot better in forty-eight hours or so, and your fever will be gone a couple of days after that.'

'What if there are complications?' Tiffany's boyfriend asked.

'Then she might need to be nursed in Intensive Care.' Holly decided not to mention the possibility of cerebral malaria—the chances were things wouldn't go that far. 'But you've come to us early enough, Tiffany, so we should be able to sort it out.'

'I hope so,' Tiffany said. 'I've got a shoot in Moscow next week.'

'Not sure you'll make that,' Holly said. 'I'm going to ask our infectious diseases specialist to come and see you. In the meantime, I'm going to start treatment—I'll give you something called quinine, and I'll also need to give you some antibiotics.' With Plasmodium falciparum it was best to assume that it was the drug-resistant type so, as well as intravenous quinine dihydrochloride, she'd give Tiffany a course of tetracycline. 'I'm going to ask one of our nurses to take some blood from you—she'll be wearing a gown, mask and gloves, but that's standard procedure and nothing to get worried about.' She patted Tiffany's arm. 'We'll get you feeling better shortly.'

She left the cubicle; Cody was the first nurse she saw. 'Cody, can you do some bloods for me? Tiffany Baker in Cubicle Three. But you'll need to barrier-nurse her as I think it's malaria.'

Cody nodded. 'Full blood count, Us and Es, and blood culture?'

'Plus thick and thin films—we might have to repeat them. Warn the lab it's potentially an infectious disease. And I'd better fill in a form for the Public Health lot after I've spoken to Infectious Diseases and got Tiffany admitted.' She smiled. 'Oh, and I could do with a urine test and an HCG test as well.'

'Right-oh.' Cody smiled back at her.

The rest of Holly's shift contained the more usual cases in an emergency department—deep lacerations that needed cleaning and suturing, sprains, suspected fractures, and removing tiny objects from the ears or noses of toddlers. She did the handover, changed and walked home.

The curtains were drawn and the light was on: it felt strange, yet welcoming. The feeling intensified when she opened the door and caught the distinctive scent of jacket potatoes and a hearty casserole. And one of her favourite CDs was playing.

She leaned against the doorjamb in the kitchen. David was chopping up fruit for a pudding, humming along to the CD. It was as if he'd always been there. Always lived with her.

If this was the future, she liked it. A lot.

'Need a hand?' she asked.

He looked up and smiled. 'No. Sit down. How was your shift?'

'OK. I had a case you'd have liked—malaria.'

'How bad?'

'If I say "Thailand"…'

He grimaced. 'That probably means drug-resistant Plasmodium falciparum—and the possibility of it becoming cerebral malaria.' Cerebral malaria was a complication which could lead to seizures, coma and even death. 'Ouch. In that case…' He reached into the fridge and poured her a glass of wine. 'Here.'

She smiled. 'Thanks. You know, I could get used to this—being waited on, hand and foot.'

'Only if we worked on different shifts. And just imagine if you were on nights and I was on earlies.'

'And we never got a day off together.' She pulled a face. 'So, um, you've been busy this afternoon?'

'Mmm-hmm. I called my landlord. Said I couldn't live with purple and orange paint any more.' He shrugged. 'It was a furnished place, so it didn't take long for me to pack.'

'So is that your CD or mine you're playing?'

'Yours. I just did my clothes today. I put most of them in the spare room. So I'm not invading your space.'

Holly set her glass back on the table. 'You're not invading my space, David. We're sharing.'

'It's your house.'

'And I'm happy to share it with you,' she said softly. 'And we're not going to do the "it should have been like this" thing either. We're different people now. We've had different experiences; maybe we even have different outlooks on some things. But I want to be with you.'

'And I want to be with you.'

'So if you think I've got too many clothes and there isn't enough room for yours, just say so.'

'Actually, I think *I'll* be the wardrobe hog,' he admitted wryly.

'Just don't tell me that your shoe habit's like Jude's,' she teased.

'No. But she told me where to buy the better-than-chocolate.'

Holly's smile broadened. 'I note that you didn't call it better-than-sex.'

David pulled her out of the chair and into his arms, and kissed her thoroughly. 'That's because I know it isn't. Not when the sex happens to be with a certain Holly Jones.' He kissed her again.

'Can I remind you that I've just come off duty? And I'm starving.'

He grinned. 'OK. I'll feed you first. And then I'll give you a foot massage.'

And she knew what would happen after the massage. 'Sounds perfect,' Holly said with a smile.

Life definitely didn't get any better than this.

On Wednesday evening, David changed swiftly after his shift and raced over to the hospital social club. He found

Holly at the back of a roomful of people and manoeuvred her into a quiet corner. 'Hi.'

'Hi, yourself.'

'Come here.' He stood behind Holly, his hands linked over her stomach, and pulled her back against him. 'Jude's got a fabulous voice,' he said, looking towards the stage.

'Yeah. I think Zo's next move is to persuade her into making a CD. We could play it on the hospital radio, sell it to visitors, that sort of thing.'

He leaned his head against hers. 'This is what it should have been like at Southampton. You and me in the Students' Union, listening to a band after a hard day's lectures.'

She stiffened slightly. 'Well, it didn't work out like that.'

He pulled her closer. No way was he going to let her freeze him out. Not now. 'I know. But it's going to work this time round.' They were living together. Doing what they should have done years ago. He nibbled her earlobe. 'So now I've moved in...are we going public?'

Holly twisted in his arms, reached up and kissed him. Very thoroughly.

When they broke the kiss, a voice said beside them, 'Thank God for that.' Kieran pretended to mop his brow. 'I don't have to watch what I'm saying any more in case my wife carries out her threat.'

Holly rolled her eyes. 'Oh, honestly. David, this is Kieran Bailey—'

'Jude's husband. We've met,' David said.

'Course you have.' The emergency department staff knew nearly everyone in the hospital, because of referrals to other departments. Holly gave an embarrassed smile.

'So what threat is this, Kieran?' David asked.

'You don't want to know,' Holly said hurriedly, remembering what Jude and Zoe had told her. *No sex ever, ever again, if they allow a single word to escape.*

Kieran laughed. 'Holly, this must be the first time I've ever seen you blush. It's probably a hospital first, come to think of it.'

'Featherboard guitar,' Holly retorted.

Kieran groaned. 'I'm never going to live that down, am I?'

'Live what down?' David asked.

'I serenaded Jude in the street. Except I can't sing. So my sister made me a featherboard guitar and I mimed it.'

'Ah, so this was the public proposal Hol told me about.' David raised an eyebrow. 'The reason why Hol won't let me kiss her outside her front door.'

'Twitching curtains,' Kieran said. 'Though my sister spotted you bringing Holly some flowers.'

'And told him. And *he* told Jude, Zo and Brad,' Holly said in disgust.

'Ah. But then Jude and Zoe told us if we breathed a word—' Kieran began.

'Enough.' Holly held her hands up in surrender. 'But it worked.'

'Be warned,' Kieran said darkly to David. 'They plot when they're together. Like the three witches.'

Holly grinned. 'Four, actually. Tess is usually in on things as well.'

'My sister. Holly's neighbour,' Kieran explained. 'Who's dying to meet you, David. I think she's planning to paint spots on Charlie's face so she can rush round and do the ''Help me, Doctor'' bit and get introduced.'

David chuckled. 'Is she here tonight?'

'No—it clashed with one of her classes. She's finishing her design course part time,' Kieran explained.

'OK. Hint taken. Tomorrow, I promise, we'll drop in and see her before we go on night duty,' Holly said.

'That's the thing about London City General,' David said, when Kieran had left to order a drink for Jude. 'You get the rush of working in a busy city department—but it feels almost like a cottage hospital, because everyone knows everyone else and looks out for them.'

'Best of all worlds.'

He tightened his arms round her. 'Everything I want is right here in my arms.'

'Me, too,' she said softly. 'Me, too.'

CHAPTER NINE

ON MONDAY night Holly reached Giovanni's before Zoe and Judith. She ordered a bottle of wine and a bottle of sparkling water, and leafed through a medical journal while she waited for her friends to turn up.

'Holls, you're an angel,' Judith said, sliding into her seat and pouring a glass of wine. 'Aren't you having any?'

'I thought I'd wait for you two,' Holly said.

'Well, hurry up and drink.' Judith poured a glass of wine for Holly. 'Zo and I are buying champagne tonight.'

'Why?' Holly gave her a speculative look. 'Are you going to make me a godmother?'

'Not yet.' Judith's eyes sparkled wickedly. 'No. We're celebrating seeing our best friend happy at last.'

'Definitely,' Zoe said, joining them at the table and clearly overhearing the last part of Judith's speech. 'If it was anyone else, I'd ask if they were absolutely sure they wanted to move in with the man of their dreams *quite* so quickly.'

'But you're picky about who you date, let alone anything else,' Judith added. 'Therefore you must be absolutely sure.'

'Mmm.' Holly sucked in a breath. 'Actually, there's something I didn't tell you. I knew David from school.'

Zoe and Judith glanced at each other. 'Was he the one who made you wary of men?' Zoe asked.

Holly rested her elbows on the table and propped her chin on her clasped hands. Yes. Of course he was. But if she told her best friends that, she'd also have to tell them

116

why. Tell them about the miscarriage. Then they'd start worrying: and there was no need. 'It was a long time ago.' She shrugged. 'And it feels right this time round.'

'If you're sure, that's all that matters,' Judith said. 'He seems nice. Kieran liked him, too.'

Holly squirmed. 'Can we change the subject? Please?'

'Sure,' Zoe said. 'Nice dress, Holls.'

Judith made a show of looking at Holly's feet. 'And shoes. Jimmy Choos, unless I'm mistaken.'

'You should know—you're the Queen of Shoes,' Zoe teased.

'Welcome to the real world, Holls.' Judith beamed. 'Excellent. I have someone new to go shoe-shopping with.'

'And this is the—what?—third time we've ever known our Holls wear a dress?' Zoe asked.

'Apart from a bridesmaid's dress—and she was dying to ask us both if she could have a trouser suit instead,' Judith teased.

Holly folded her arms. 'What is this? Torment Holly night?'

'Just getting our own back for all those comments about walking down the aisle in a meringue.' Zoe leaned over and hugged her. 'Holls, you look lovely. As if you're smiling from the inside out. It's really serious between you and David, isn't it?'

'Yes. And that scares me,' Holly admitted. 'I never thought I'd even see him again. When I walked in and saw him standing there, chatting to Anna, it threw me a bit.'

'But you've sorted out whatever your differences were?' Judith asked.

'I think so. But…' Holly shivered. 'I'm just scared it'll all go wrong if I talk about it.'

'Course it won't,' Zoe reassured her. But, to Holly's relief, she changed the subject.

*   *   *

Work was more of the same—good-natured teasing and a few suggestive comments. But everyone seemed to accept immediately that Holly and David were a couple—a team outside work as well as in the department.

'Hol—can I borrow you?' David asked, catching her in the corridor. 'You're good with littlies.'

'What's the problem?'

'Fingertip amputation. Little girl, two years old, mum opened the front door to get a parcel and the back door slammed shut—but the little girl's hand was in the way.'

Holly winced as she followed him over to the cubicle. 'How many fingers?'

'Just the left middle, the mum says. She wrapped it in a clean wet tea towel and came straight here.'

'Salvageable?'

'From a quick examination of her finger, yes, I think so.'

'Want me to call someone from Plastics?'

'I can do the sutures, but I need you to help keep the little girl calm and distract her while I'm sewing.'

David introduced Holly to Dora Gregory and her mother.

'OK, Dora. I've got some very special stickers for brave little girls,' David said. 'I'm going to look at your hand and Dr Holly is going to help me make you better.'

The little girl was still sobbing, and one look at Mrs Gregory told Holly that the woman was very near losing control.

'What we're going to do is give her a digital block—that's an anaesthetic to numb her finger, and it won't cause extra swelling of the tissues,' David said. 'Then I can have a look at her finger and see what's happened.'

'Is she going to lose her finger?' Mrs Gregory asked.

'Hopefully not. In children of Dora's age, if the bone isn't crushed, we should be able to sew her fingertip back on in what we call a composite graft—all that means is that there's more than one type of tissue,' Holly explained. 'David said you wrapped the fingertip in a wet towel?'

'I didn't know what else to do,' Mrs Gregory said.

'It's exactly the right thing. Can I take a look?' Holly asked. At Mrs Gregory's nod, she unwrapped the fingertip, then rewrapped it in moist saline swabs and placed it in a sealed plastic bag. 'I'll ask the nurse to sort something out for us,' she said. To her relief, Michelle was in the corridor. 'Miche, can you get that in iced water for us, please?' she asked, handing the bag to the nurse.

'Sure. I'll bring it back in. Want me to bring cephalosporin with me?'

Cephalosporin was a broad-spectrum antibiotic which they'd need to give the little girl to prevent any nasty infections. 'And tetanus cover, please,' Holly said.

She went back into the cubicle and held the little girl's hand while David injected the block.

'Well done, Dora. You definitely deserve one of Dr David's special stickers.' She soothed the little girl.

David examined Dora's finger more closely. 'I'm going to need to remove the nail and repair it. There's a chance that the nail might not grow back,' he said. 'But the good news is, I can sew the fingertip back on. She's not going to lose it.'

'Thank God,' Mrs Gregory said, her voice filled with tears.

Michelle reappeared with the plastic bag, cephalosporin and tetanus vaccination.

'Did you know I can do balloon animals, Dora?' Holly asked. 'Shall I make you a teddy? A pink one?' At the little girl's shy nod, Holly took a modelling balloon from her pocket, blew it up and twisted it into shape. While Dora watched Holly intently, David was able to give her the antibiotics and vaccination without any fuss.

'I didn't know you did this sort of thing in the emergency department,' Mrs Gregory said.

David smiled. 'Holly's our local Superwoman. She can do anything.'

'My best friend's a paediatrician,' Holly explained, for Mrs Gregory's benefit. 'She did a fundraising thing involving balloons, and I had a crash course in them. I do a great poodle, too.'

'A *pink* poodle?' Dora asked hopefully.

'Or even a purple one, if you're a brave girl,' Holly said. She glanced at Mrs Gregory. 'You might want to look away from what David's doing,' she warned quietly. 'It's not going to hurt Dora at all because of the anaesthetic, but it doesn't look very nice.'

'I'm not very good with blood and things like that,' Mrs Gregory said, her lower lip trembling.

'You've done brilliantly today,' Holly said. 'Dora, can you sit on my lap, sweetheart?'

The little girl nodded and allowed her mother to shift her onto Holly's lap, still clutching her balloon teddy with her uninjured hand.

'Once David's done all the stitching, I'll put a dressing and a splint on Dora's hand,' Holly said. She glanced down to see that David had put a Penrose drain in and removed the nail. 'The splint rests the hand so the tissues heal faster—but we're going to need Dora to keep her hand up, roughly to the level of her heart, and keep the hand as rested as she can.' David was repairing the nail matrix with absorbable stitches. 'I know it's hard with toddlers—they love to rush about.' She smiled. 'Dora's about the same age as my neighbour's little boy, Charlie. So I'd prescribe a few videos and lots of stories over the next couple of days.

We'll also give you a sling for Dora's arm—that should help keep her hand up high enough.' She chatted easily to Dora and Mrs Gregory, until a final quick glance showed her that David had reinserted the nail plate.

He nodded to her and took over explaining the procedures to Mrs Gregory until Holly had applied a sterile dressing to Dora's finger and splinted the hand.

'Bring her back to see us in a couple of days, so we can check how she's doing. We'll give you some painkillers for her, too,' David said. 'But if she gets any pain at all, bring her straight back.'

'Oh—and try to keep the dressing dry, if you can,' Holly said.

David fished in the pocket of his white coat. 'Right, Dora. I think you've been so brave, you should have a bravery sticker *and* a purple poodle—what do you think, Holly?'

'Definitely,' she said.

The little girl's face lit up when David gave her a glittery 'bravery' sticker, then Holly made a purple balloon poodle.

'Thank you,' Mrs Gregory said.

'No problem.' David smiled back at her. When she'd left, he caught Holly round the waist and kissed her. 'To teamwork,' he said.

'Yeah. Teamwork. Nice stitching, Dr Neave.' Meticulous *and* fast. She'd been seriously impressed.

'Nice balloon work, Dr Jones. Another thing I didn't know about you.' He rubbed his nose against hers. 'Any other little talents you want to tell me about?'

She laughed and released his hold. 'No. Balloon animals and bad self-defence throws are about my limit.'

The next month was the best Holly could ever remember. The department was running smoothly, she still had her girly lunches with Zoe and Judith, and when they decided to allow their partners to attend every other Giovanni night, David fitted in as if he'd always been part of their social circle. And her house really *was* home now, with the man she loved to share it with her.

Not that either of them had mentioned the L-word. Holly had a feeling that David shared her fear it might jinx things if they actually said 'I love you'. But his heartbeat was the last thing she heard before she slept, and his face was the first thing she saw when she woke. That was the way she wanted it to stay. The two of them, together.

But on one Sunday night Holly felt distinctly odd. She splashed water onto her face, willing herself to feel more awake. She didn't usually have a problem with night duty—but then again, her life had changed a lot lately. Since David had been back in it.

Maybe that was why she was feeling so strange.

Then she had to hold onto the sink, hard, as a very nasty thought occurred to her. Her breasts had felt very tender last night. She'd been to the loo more often than usual during her shift. And she hadn't drunk coffee for days. Hadn't even wanted it.

A quick mental calculation made her feel even queasier—because her period was five weeks late. The only times she'd ever been late in the past had been because of exam pressure, and—she swallowed hard—that time she'd tried so desperately to forget, when she'd been eighteen. When her world had collapsed.

She splashed more water on her face. There was a rational explanation for all this. She was just finishing her sixth day on duty: that was why she was tired. She'd switched from coffee to water in an attempt to be healthy— and because she was drinking more water she needed to go to the loo more often. Her period was late because she'd been busy.

As for the breast tenderness…she'd think of a reason for that.

But the doubts nagged at her for the rest of the shift.

Was she pregnant?

They'd used protection. But the only one hundred per cent guaranteed protection was abstinence. A condom might have split without them realising.

And then there had been that time in the whirlpool bath. The first time. When they'd both been so carried away that… She bit her lip in disbelief. Oh, no. Not only had they not used protection, neither of them had given it a second thought afterwards. It hadn't even occurred to them that they'd taken a risk. And now it was way, way, way too late to think of the morning-after pill.

'You OK?' David asked as they left the hospital. 'You look a bit pale.'

'Just tired after night shift.' Holly smiled at him, hoping he'd take her comment at face value. Until she had it clear in her head she didn't want to talk to him about this. Didn't want to risk everything going wrong, the way it had last time.

'Home. Bed,' he directed.

'Mmm. I just want to get a couple of things from the shops on the way home. You go ahead,' she said.

'Give me a list and I'll do it,' he offered.

No. Absolutely not. She couldn't ask him something like that, out of the blue. *Get me a pint of milk and a pregnancy test, darling.* It wouldn't be fair. 'Women's stuff,' she prevaricated. It was true enough, though he'd probably think she meant tampons.

If only she did.

She kissed him goodbye outside the supermarket.

'I'll have the kettle on ready for when you get home,' he promised.

Holly bought milk, bread and a double-pack of pregnancy test sticks. Hell. This was just like the last time she'd done this: bought the test kit secretly and worried herself sick that the result would be positive.

She steeled herself. This time it would be different. The test wouldn't be positive. It *couldn't* be.

But supposing it was? Her stomach lurched. Would David back out on her again? Of course not. He hadn't even known she was pregnant last time. This time he'd stand by her.

He had to.

Even so, she ended up hiding the test sticks in her handbag rather than in the shopping bag, and threw away the receipt before she got home. She didn't want him knowing before she was ready to tell him. And she might be panicking over nothing, seeing signs that just weren't there. 'Fresh bread,' she said, waving the loaf at him.

'Excellent.' He grabbed butter from the fridge. 'I've made coffee.'

Coffee? Holly fought back the nausea. 'Thanks, but I'll pass.' At his look of surprise, she added, 'Caffeine before bed—I'll never get any sleep.'

'Hot blackcurrant, then?'

She wasn't sure she could handle anything except water. But that was silly. It was all psychological. Of course she wasn't pregnant. 'To be honest, I'm wiped. I'm going straight to bed.'

'I'll join you.' His eyes narrowed when she failed to give him even a lukewarm response. 'Hol, is anything wrong?'

'No,' she lied. 'I'm just tired.'

'Right.' The next thing she knew, he'd picked her up and was carrying her up the stairs.

'Put me down.'

'Sure.' He set her on her feet next to the bed and closed the curtains. Before she had a chance to think about anything, her clothes were lying in a heap on the floor.

'David...' She really, really didn't want to make love. Not with this knot of fear and uncertainty in her stomach.

'Shh.' He pulled the duvet back and patted the mattress. 'Lie face down.'

'What?'

'Lie face down,' he directed softly. 'Then close your eyes.'

She was beyond arguing. She felt the mattress give, and then his hands on her shoulders. Soothing. Kneading the tension away, his touch firm yet gentle.

She wanted to cry, wanted to hug him, wanted to sleep, all at once.

She was asleep before he'd finished.

Later that day, Holly woke, curled in David's arms. His hand was splayed across her stomach, holding her against him. It felt so good, lying here with him. Protected. Cocooned from the world, just the two of them.

Or was it three?

She had to know. She really, really had to know.

Slowly, carefully, she wriggled out from his arms without waking him, then pulled her dressing-gown on. She crept downstairs, avoiding the creaky stair, and took the test kit out of her handbag. She refilled the kettle and switched it on—just in case David woke and wondered what she was doing downstairs—then went into the downstairs toilet and did the test.

Funny how a minute could seem so short at work and so long right now. The seconds seemed to slip into hours as she waited to find out the truth.

Please, let there be only one blue line.

One blue line appeared, proving that she'd done the test correctly.

Please, let there be only one blue line.

Her stomach lurched as the liquid seeped up to the second window.

Please, let there be only one blue line.

As the second line became visible, she was promptly sick.

She shoved the test stick and the spare in her pocket, rinsed her mouth and splashed her face with cold water.

It was a mistake. It *had* to be a mistake. A false positive. They happened. She *knew* they happened. She couldn't be pregnant.

She buried the packaging in the bin, then made David a cup of coffee—trying not to gag at the scent—and took it up to him.

'Thanks,' he said sleepily.

How was she going to tell him?

It must be a mistake. Maybe the test had come from a faulty batch. She'd try the other one first. If that was positive, then she'd have to tell him. 'I'm going to have a shower and wash my hair,' she said.

He raised an eyebrow. 'Want me to wash your back?'

'No. Have a lie-in.'

She grabbed her clothes and locked the bathroom door behind her. She did the second test—then, unable to bear watching it, stepped into the shower. When she'd wrapped her wet hair in a towel and dried herself, she looked at the second test.

Then at the first, just to make sure.

There was no mistake. The tests were both positive.

She drew in a shuddering breath. She and David had only

just got back together…and now she was pregnant. How was she going to tell him?

The question that really scared her was how he was going to react. Shock, disbelief, delight? She really didn't know. Would he stand by her this time, or would he back away, feeling trapped?

She dressed, shoved the tests into the pocket of her jeans and headed downstairs. She wasn't even sure she could handle dry toast, but she made some for David, buttered it and took it upstairs.

'Wow. Thank you. What did I do to deserve being spoiled?' he asked, smiling at her and sitting up against a pile of pillows.

'Nothing.'

He patted the bed beside him. 'You look terrible, Hol. Is it just the tail end of nights, or are you going down with the virus that seems to be knocking everyone out?'

This was her cue. She had to tell him. Now. 'David, we need to talk.'

He frowned and put his toast to one side. 'What's up?'

She took a deep, shuddering breath. 'My period's late.'

'Probably the stress of me moving in and hogging all your wardrobe space,' he said lightly.

She shook her head. 'I'm pregnant.'

He frowned. 'You can't be. We've used protection.'

'Except that first time. In the whirlpool bath.' She swallowed miserably.

He looked at her in shock. 'You're right. I should have…' His voice tailed off and he shook his head. 'Oh, hell. I didn't even think.'

'Neither did I. And it only takes once, doesn't it?'

'Are you absolutely sure, Hol?'

'Yes.' She pulled the tests from her pocket and handed them to him.

David stared at the two little white sticks. Each stick had two windows, and each window had a blue line. Two lines to confirm that the test had been performed correctly, and two lines to confirm that the test was positive.

They were going to have a baby.

No. There had to be some kind of mistake. It couldn't be true. They'd only just got back together—they'd hardly had time to rediscover each other yet. They weren't *ready* for a baby.

'Say something.'

He could hear the unshed tears in her voice. Hell. She needed him. Of course she did, and he'd be there for her. But he didn't know what to say. 'Hol...' He raked his hand through his hair. Honesty. He had to be honest with her. 'I don't know what to say. I didn't expect... This is...' Hell. Worse and worse. He was completely incoherent and she was worried sick. Maybe he should cut to the chase. The most important thing. 'Look, of course we'll get married.' Just as they hadn't last time.

Not that he'd even *known* about the baby last time.

But marriage... Even the word scared him silly. 'I know my track record's not good, and my marriage to Alyson barely lasted three years.' Ha. And that was half as long again as his relationship with Holly the first time round. At least he and Alyson hadn't had children, so when they'd split up they'd only hurt each other. If it didn't work out between him and Holly this time round it would be a lot more serious. There was the baby to consider.

He'd just have to make it work. 'But I'll stand by you. Of course I'll stand by you.'

She was staring at him as if he had two heads. As if he'd said something wrong. But...what? He'd offered to marry her, give the baby his name. Wasn't that what she expected?

'I'm going for a run.'

He shook his head. 'I don't think you should use the treadmill. Not in your condition.'

Holly's retort was extremely short and extremely rude. Before he had the chance to take in what she'd said, she'd slammed the bedroom door behind her. Another bang, a few seconds later, heralded the front door closing.

He rushed to the sash window. But the wooden frame was slightly swollen and refused to give. By the time he'd managed to push the sash up and stuck his head out to call to her, she was out of sight.

Hell. He had no idea where she'd gone, but he had to find her. He pulled his clothes on, picked up his keys and left the house. Stuff the burglar alarm. He couldn't care less if a thief stripped the whole house bare. Things could be replaced; people couldn't. Right now, the important thing was to find Holly, bring her home and tell her everything was going to be all right.

And if he said it loudly enough, he might even believe it himself.

CHAPTER TEN

OF COURSE we'll get married.

Holly was fuming as she stomped along the pavement, oblivious to her surroundings. What had David expected—applause for his noble gesture? It wasn't as if she'd got pregnant on purpose! As for trapping him into marriage, that hadn't even entered her mind.

My track record isn't good. Yeah, she knew that. They'd been together for a little under two years the first time round. His marriage hadn't lasted very long either. But did that mean every relationship he'd ever have would break up? Talk about a pathetic excuse.

And why had he focused on *himself* and his feelings? What about her? What about 'I love you, Holly'? What about 'Wow, we're going to have a baby'? But no. She'd got, 'I'll stand by you.' The dutiful response.

She clenched her hands. *Duty.* She definitely didn't want a baby with someone who was only staying with her out of duty. Her hands were so tense they felt as if they were about to explode. Maybe she should have taken up something like kick-boxing, so she could go and let off steam any time she needed to. Or even ordinary boxing: sparring with a punchball would be great right now. She could knock it into next week and pretend it was David's stupid, dutiful smile.

Though physical contact sports weren't a good idea when you were pregnant. So the trainer would probably have barred her anyway.

Frustration rippled through her. How could she have

been such an idiot? Hadn't she learned anything from the past? David had let her down before. Yes, he'd claimed he would have been there for her if he'd known, but how could she be sure he was telling the truth? Maybe he really *had* known, and he'd just weaseled out of his responsibility.

He'd said he'd support her, but she had a nasty feeling he'd weasel out of it this time round, too.

A hooter blasted, and she stepped back onto the kerb as the car screeched to a halt. The driver wound the window down and yelled at her, 'You ought to look where you're going, you stupid cow!'

She flinched, knowing the rebuke was well deserved. She was so wound up she'd forgotten where she was. She'd stepped off the pavement without thinking and if that driver's reactions hadn't been so fast she'd have been a pancake. 'Sorry, mate,' she called back.

'Bloody women,' the driver growled, and drove off with a screech of tyres.

Holly scrubbed at her face with the back of her hand. She was *not* going to cry about nearly getting run over. She was *not* going to cry over David Neave. She didn't need him and his magnanimous gestures. In fact, she didn't need him, full stop. Her baby deserved better than a father who was only going to be there out of duty. And she was going to tell him so right now.

But when she got home the house was empty. He'd locked the door but he hadn't bothered putting the burglar alarm on, which showed just how responsible he was. As in *not*.

Holly mooched around for the next hour, unable to settle to anything. She couldn't concentrate enough to catch up on her pile of journals, she really couldn't face anything to eat and she couldn't find the right kind of music to soothe her mood—everything seemed either too soppy or reminded her of times with David that she wanted to forget. *Needed* to forget.

Because their relationship wasn't going anywhere. Not any more. She was better off on her own.

She tried cleaning, but that didn't help—the chemicals made her feel nauseous, to the point where she was being sick in the downstairs toilet when she heard the front door close.

It was hard to be dignified when you were vomiting. Hard to have a conversation, even. Why couldn't he have delayed his return by another ten minutes, so she could at least have pretended to be poised? she thought in disgust.

'Holly?' David called.

She washed her face and reappeared in the kitchen. She couldn't talk to him now. 'I need to clean my teeth,' she said, barely moving her lips in case she was sick again.

'Are you OK?'

She hoped her glare would tell him just how stupid that question was.

'Do you want me to get you some water? Dry toast?'

'Forget it,' she snapped, and went to clean her teeth.

He followed her upstairs and hovered in the bathroom doorway. 'Hol, I was worried about you.'

Yeah, right. She'd heard that one before. She ignored him and concentrated on scrubbing the foul taste from her mouth.

'I tried to follow you but you'd vanished by the time I got downstairs. I went looking for you—obviously I went the wrong way because I couldn't find you.'

Well, three cheers for Mr Hero. She spat viciously into the sink.

'Holly.' He handed her a towel and took the toothbrush from her hand. 'We need to talk.'

She couldn't argue with that. 'Yes.'

'Come and sit down.'

With him? She didn't think so. What she had to say wouldn't take long, anyway. She leaned against the door-jamb and folded her arms. 'I need space.'

'What?'

Why was he staring at her as if she'd grown two heads? 'I need space,' she repeated. 'I had a lot of time to think while I was out. I'd like you to move out.'

He stared at her, disbelief written all over his face. 'You want me to move out?'

'Yes.' How much clearer could she be?

'Hol, I know you're upset, but don't blank me like this. We need to talk about what's happening.'

'There's nothing to talk about.'

He gave a mirthless laugh. 'Oh, I think there is. You're pregnant with *my* baby.'

'I need space, David,' she said again.

'You're angry with me. Of course you are. I behaved like an idiot when you told me. But, Hol, remember that I'd just finished a six-day stretch. Two nights. I hadn't had enough sleep to take in what you were saying.'

She'd just finished a six-day stretch, too. Two nights. She'd taken it in—she'd *had* to—so why hadn't he?

'Holly, we need to talk about what you want.'

She lifted her chin. 'I've already told you. I want space.'

'I meant, where the baby's concerned.'

'That's not up for discussion.'

He rolled his eyes. 'That's your hormones talking. Come and sit down. I'll get you a glass of water and some cream crackers to settle your stomach, and we can talk.'

She stared at him. 'Aren't you listening? There's nothing to say.'

'Funny, I've got a huge list in my head. Starting with having a dating scan, making an appointment with your midwife, discussing things with Sue to make sure you don't go anywhere near any X-rays or dangerous patients and your workload isn't too heavy.' He started ticking things off against his fingers. 'Then there's where and when we're going to get married, what sort of birth you want, antenatal classes, what colour you want me to paint the nursery, whether we're going to stay here or look for a bigger house. Shall I go on?'

She'd wanted support, not a steamroller. Where was 'I love you, Holly, we'll get through this together'? David wasn't planning to support her, he was planning to take over! His list might contain sops to her wants, but she'd bet good money that he'd push her towards the option *he* wanted on every single point. He wasn't going to give her any time to let things sink in, time to think about the possibilities and the options. The doctor in him was taking over, wanting results right now.

She had to stop him. Fast. There was only one thing she could think of that would do it. 'You're assuming that I'm going to keep the baby.'

David felt the air whoosh out of his lungs, as if she'd just sucker-punched him. Holly was planning to have a termination? She was seriously intending to get rid of the little life they'd created? OK, so they hadn't planned to have a baby, at least not yet. They hadn't even talked about it. Finding out she was pregnant had been a hell of a shock. But was she *really* going to have a termination, without even discussing it with him first?

He swallowed hard. Maybe he'd misheard her. Holly wasn't like that. She wasn't that ruthless…was she? But right now her eyes were like flints, a hard dark grey, challenging him to say a single word to contradict her.

Maybe he'd got it wrong after all. Hadn't she told him

herself she wanted a senior registrar's job next year? A baby would capsize her career plans, so if she wanted to keep to her schedule, she'd have to get rid of the baby.

Their baby.

If she loved him, she'd be prepared to talk. To compromise. To work out a solution together. But she'd made it perfectly clear that she wasn't giving him a say in this. She wanted everything *her* way. She wanted space. She didn't want to keep their baby. She wanted him to move out.

And then a truly nasty thought occurred to him. Supposing she hadn't told him the complete truth about what had happened all those years ago? Supposing it hadn't been a miscarriage at all but a termination?

She hadn't discussed it then, and she wasn't discussing it now. Same old story: her ambition came first. He really hadn't learned anything at all, had he? Last time she'd put him through the wringer. This time she was doing exactly the same. She'd made it very clear that she didn't love him and he wasn't good enough to be the father to her baby. Last time, he could understand the logic—he was from a poor family, hers were posh, and they'd been little more than kids themselves—but things were different now. He didn't have an accent any more, he was a qualified doctor, *and* he was Holly's senior at work. No way was he not good enough for her, in her family's eyes.

But if that was how she saw it, let her have what she wanted. He wasn't going to beg her. She wasn't the only one who could be proud. If she didn't want him, he'd just walk away. 'I'll give you space, Holly.' For good. 'I'll stay in a hotel tonight. I'll find myself somewhere else to live tomorrow and move my things out.'

'Fine. I'll make sure I'm out tomorrow afternoon. Post my keys back through the letterbox when you've finished.'

'Fine.'

And that was it.

All over.

It didn't take long to pack a few clothes. She didn't stay to watch him. When he paused in the hallway and glanced through the door to the living room, he saw her curled up on the sofa, skimming through a medical journal and making notes. As if nothing had happened.

Unbelievable.

He hadn't fallen in love with a confident, assertive woman. Far from it. Holly Jones was everything they said she was: scary and unapproachable. If she had a heart—which he was seriously beginning to doubt—it was armour-plated. Just like the rest of her. He'd been kidding himself this past month or so. He'd wanted so desperately to believe that he'd found his soul mate. That she loved him just as much as he loved her but was too scared to say it. And, fool that he was, he'd thought he could win her round. Teach her to trust. Teach her to love.

But Holly was incapable of love. She was nothing but ambition made flesh and bone. Just like last time, he'd been enough to amuse her for a while. Now she was bored, she didn't want the inconvenience of pregnancy, and she wanted out of their relationship.

Well, that was fine by him.

He didn't bother saying goodbye. He just walked out of her house and out of her life. Tomorrow he'd find himself another flat and ask Sue to change his shifts so he didn't have to see Holly any more than he had to.

When the front door closed, Holly put down the journal she hadn't been able to read, dropped her pen and the spiral-bound notebook containing pages of meaningless doodles and curled up in the foetal position.

David was gone.

She'd asked him to go and he'd left. He hadn't even made a token protest. Which only went to prove just how little he cared about her. If he'd loved her, really loved her, he wouldn't have tried to make demands or insist on talking things over that very second. Instead, he would have held her. Told her he loved her and it was going to be all right, that he'd be with her no matter what and they'd work it out together.

But he hadn't.

And nothing was ever going to be all right again.

The tears trickled down her face unchecked. She was doing the right thing. She *knew* she was. David had offered to marry her, yes—but it hadn't been because he loved her. Without love, their marriage couldn't last. It was better to make a clean break now, before their child got hurt.

Except it didn't feel like a clean break. It felt as if her heart had been torn out with a rusty spoon, jagged edges and bruising everywhere.

Some time later, she bathed her reddened eyes and washed her face. She didn't want to be on her own any more tonight. She needed company. With any luck, Zoe and Jude wouldn't be on a late shift. Maybe they could go to Giovanni's or to see a film. Anything. She'd even sit through the kind of slush she hated if it meant she would be with people who really cared about her.

She picked up the phone. To her relief, Zoe answered within two rings. 'Hi, Zo. It's Holly. I wondered if you fancied a pizza or the pictures tonight?'

'Holls, I'd love to, but I can't—Brad's got tickets for that concert at the Barbican tonight. We're on our way out right now, actually. How about tomorrow night?'

'Yeah, maybe.' Holly hoped that she sounded a lot more cheerful than she felt. She wasn't going to spoil things for

Zoe by sobbing down the phone. There was time for that tomorrow. 'Have a good time.'

'Cheers, we will. I'll ring you tomorrow.'

Holly replaced the receiver, but she couldn't bring herself to call Jude. One 'no' was more than enough for her right now. She stayed curled on the sofa for a long, long time—she wasn't sure quite how long—and then the doorbell rang.

Hope leapt in her stomach. Maybe it was David. Maybe he'd come back to tell her he loved her and he didn't want them to fight any more. Maybe...

She opened the door to see her best friend standing there. 'Jude!' She pinned a smile to her face and hoped that Judith wouldn't spot it straight off as a fake. 'Hi. I wasn't expecting you. Come in.'

'Zo rang me from her mobile. She said you sounded...' Judith winced. 'Um. Well, not your normal self. So here I am, bearing gianduja.'

As soon as Judith opened the box and the scent of the gianduja hit her, Holly bolted for the bathroom and retched miserably. And then a cool cloth was wiping her forehead and a glass of cold water was being pressed into her hand.

'Are you coming down with a bug, Hol?' Judith asked.

She couldn't lie. Not to her best friend. 'No.'

Jude was an obstetrician, so Holly knew exactly what was coming next. 'Are you pregnant?'

'Yes.'

'Right.' Judith gently ushered her into the dining room. 'What do you want me to get you? Toast? An apple?'

Holly shook her head, very slightly—anything more would send her running back to the bathroom. 'Can't face anything.'

'OK. Does David know?'

'Yes.'

'Then where is he?'

Holly took a shuddering breath. 'Gone.'

'What?' Judith's eyes widened. 'How could he desert you at a time like this? I'll kill him!'

'No. I told him to leave.' Holly explained the whole sorry story to Judith, leaving nothing out, even the truth about why her gap year hadn't worked out: because it had been before her exams, not after, as a result of her miscarriage.

'Oh, Holls.' Judith held her close. 'I don't know what to say. But whatever you decide to do I'll be with you all the way. So will Zo.'

So accepting. So unlike the reaction she'd had from David—and even more unlike the reaction Holly knew she'd get from her mother. Laura Jones would throw the epitome of all hissy fits.

'How pregnant are you?'

'Um…my period is five weeks late.' She should have been able to work it out, but her brain was full of cotton wool and refused to do the calculation for her.

Jude came to the rescue. 'So that's nine weeks gestation, counting from the first day of your last period. You've got plenty of time to think about what you want.'

'I told David I was going to have a termination.'

Jude squeezed her hand. 'If that's what you really want, it's not a problem. I'm not going to judge you and neither's Zoe. I can help you arrange it, if you want me to.'

'I don't think I can do it. Not after…' Holly swallowed, thinking of the miscarriage. Of the screaming sense of loss she'd felt for months afterwards—still felt, some days, when it crept up on her at an unguarded moment. 'My baby would have been eleven now. At senior school.' She sniffed. 'I was supposed to be a village GP.'

'Holls, it wasn't to be. And if things *had* worked out like that London City General would be without the best emergency registrar they've ever had.'

'And I'd never have met you or Zo.'

'Exactly. There's a silver lining to nearly everything. It'll all work out. Trust me.' Jude smiled at her. 'So, if you're keeping the baby I know an obstetrician who'd be only too happy to add you to her list. Unless you'd rather have Kieran, as he's a bit more senior and, um, didn't need Zoe to coach him through his exams.'

Tears welled in Holly's eyes and splashed over. 'Jude, I can't think of anyone I'd rather have looking after me than you.'

'Come and see me tomorrow—at work. We'll say we're having lunch and you're early because your watch is fast. I'll pinch Keiran's office and the portable scanner and we'll do a dating scan. That way, the grapevine won't have a clue until you're ready to tell the world. And if anyone guesses I'll get Kieran to read the Riot Act about patient confidentiality. Anyone who breaks it will have to listen to him sing, and nobody's going to risk that.'

Holly smiled through her tears. 'Oh, Jude. I don't deserve this.'

'Course you do. Who was it who put me straight when I thought Tess was Kieran's wife? Who was it who persuaded Giovanni's to do a take-away especially for me? That's what friends are for.' Judith handed Holly a tissue. 'Have you eaten?'

Holly shook her head.

'I'll fix you dinner.' Judith gave her a mischievous smile. 'And, no, I'm not going out for a take-away. You need something nutritious that has almost no scent and a fairly bland taste so it's not going to make you feel rough. Knowing you, there's a ton of fruit in your kitchen, so I'll start there. Stay put and I'll be back in a mo.'

Holly dashed the tears away with the back of her hand. 'Why is everyone taking over?'

'Be-ca-u-se—' Judith sang the word, making it into four syllables '—you're pregnant. And I'm an obstetrician and that means I can boss you about.' She grinned. 'It's only for the next seven months, so I'm going to make the most of it!'

Three minutes later, she returned with a plate on which she'd arranged slices of apple, melon, hard cheese and dry crackers. 'You need to get into the habit of eating dried apricots—half a dozen or so a day. It's good for your iron levels and it'll stop any potential problems with constipation.'

'I've never, ever seen you boss anyone around like this at work,' Holly grumbled.

'You're a special case.' Judith gave her a broad wink.

'Thanks, Jude. And for doing all this for me.'

'No problem. Though I'm going to extract a promise from you. If you're worried about anything—I mean *anything*, no matter how small or stupid it seems to you—I want you to ring me. Any time, even if it's three o'clock in the morning.'

Holly nodded. 'Thanks.'

'I want a *proper* promise, Holls,' Judith insisted.

'I promise I'll ring you if I'm worried about anything. Even if it's feeble.' Holly drew the shape of a cross over her heart. 'Cross my heart.'

'Good.' Judith gave Holly a speculative look. 'You told David you're having a termination. Are you going to tell him you've changed your mind?'

'No.'

'Don't you think he'll notice? You work together. OK, you might be able to hide the bump until about eighteen weeks, but after that you'll show and it'll be obvious.'

'Jude, there's no point in telling him. He doesn't love me, and I don't want him to stay with me out of duty. We'll end up resenting each other, even hating each other, and I don't want that.'

'Do you love him?'

Holly nodded. 'I don't think I ever really got over him, to be honest. But one-way relationships are never going to work. So it's over.'

It was so easy to say. But inside she was dying slowly. Lonely and scared, just as she'd been at eighteen. Crying her heart out over David Neave and wishing he loved her as much as she loved him. Wishing that she had enough love for both of them, so it wouldn't matter that he didn't feel the same about her.

'His stuff's still here,' Judith pointed out.

'Only temporarily. He's picking it up tomorrow.'

'Maybe you should give each other time to cool off, then talk to each other. The baby must have been a shock for both of you—you probably both said things you didn't mean, because neither of you were thinking straight.'

Holly pushed her plate away. 'Too late, Jude. And please don't think that you can talk him round either.'

Judith bit her lip. 'Oh. Was it that obvious?'

'No, but I know you. And I appreciate the thought. It's just…' Holly sighed. 'I can't believe I let him mess my life up again so easily.'

'You're not on your own, Holls. You've got me, Zo, Kieran and Brad. And Tess.'

'I know.' Holly brushed away a tear. 'I can't handle all this weeping business. Are pregnant women *always* this wet?'

Judith chuckled. 'It's your hormones, love. When they've settled down again you'll be fine. You'll be blooming in the second trimester. Three or four weeks' time, you'll be feeling on top of the world.'

It sounded good, but Holly couldn't see it happening. Right now she didn't think she'd ever feel on top of the world again. Not without David.

Maybe tomorrow would be better, once he'd moved out properly.

Or maybe not.

She'd just have to get used to coping on her own. She'd done it perfectly well for the last twelve years. So why did it seem so hard now?

CHAPTER ELEVEN

DAVID rang the doorbell. When there was no answer, he let himself in.

Home.

In the month since he'd moved in, Holly's Victorian terrace had felt more like home than any other place he'd ever lived—the house where he'd grown up, the house where he'd lived during his marriage to Alyson, even his place in Newcastle. Home, because that was where Holly was. Where his *heart* was.

But she'd made it clear that she didn't want him.

He'd half hoped she might be there. That she'd give him a chance to talk things through properly now they'd both had time to cool off. But maybe it was for the best that she wasn't: another row would make the chasm between them gape even wider. He unlocked the back door and dumped the large bunch of gerberas straight in the dustbin. Even if he left them for her, he knew she'd throw them out, so he might as well save them both some time.

It didn't take long to pack, simply because he couldn't care less about folding his clothes neatly. His books and CDs were next—in plastic carrier bags rather than boxes, because it really didn't matter any more. The things he'd bought for the house he left—he couldn't face all the memories around him if he took them with him. If Holly didn't want them, she could throw them out. Just like she'd thrown him out.

'Ah, Holly. If only you'd loved me as much as I love you,' he said, the words ripped straight from his soul. If only she'd been prepared to let him past the walls she'd built round herself.

They'd made a baby together. But instead of bringing them closer it had torn them apart. It had shown him the truth about Holly: her career came first, last and always. A baby would have been in the way, just like he was. Right now, she was probably arranging the termination, maybe even having the procedure done. And it hurt like hell that she'd refused even to discuss it with him first.

She'd rejected him and she'd rejected his baby.

'If only,' he said softly, and piled the rest of his belongings into the van he'd hired for the day. He pushed her keys through the letterbox.

And that was it. Over. All over.

'Ready?' Judith asked as Holly settled back on the couch.

Holly nodded. 'Ready.'

'Holls, do you think you should...?' Zoe began tentatively.

'No,' Holly said quietly, guessing exactly what her best friend was thinking. 'I'm not going to ring David and ask him if he wants to see the scan. Yes, he'd come straight up here, but it would be because he thought he *ought* to be here, not because he wanted to be here. There's a difference.' All the difference in the world.

'OK.' Zoe squeezed Holly's hand. 'I'll stop nagging.'

'Good.' Holly gave her best attempt at a smile.

'This will feel cold—it's better in the antenatal clinic because it's so warm in the ultrasound rooms that the gel actually reaches room temperature,' Judith said.

Holly gasped as Judith smeared the cold gel onto her stomach.

'All righty.' Judith picked up the scanner head. 'Let's take a look at my godchild.'

'*Our* godchild,' Zoe corrected with a smile. 'Holls, this is so exciting. Our first baby!'

Second, actually, Holly corrected silently. Though she hadn't seen a scan the first time round. She hadn't had enough time.

As Judith ran the scanner head over Holly's stomach and the ultrasound picture appeared on the screen, Holly had to blink back tears. 'That's my baby?'

'Yep. That dark area's your placenta. Two arms, two legs, feet and hands look fine, the heartbeat's nice and steady.'

'It's whizzing about like a tornado,' Holly said, transfixed by the picture.

'What do you expect, with Superwoman as his mum and Hurricane Zoe as his godmother?' Judith teased.

'His? You can tell the sex *this* early nowadays?' Holly asked.

Judith shook her head. 'Not from an ultrasound until about twenty weeks, but I call all babies "he". It's a bad habit, I know—I just can't stand calling babies "it".' She paused the picture. 'I should be able to get a good measurement here. Crown to rump length nineteen millimetres.' She didn't even have to check on the chart taped to the scanner to confirm it. 'Yep, you're about nine weeks.' She smiled. 'We're going to have to do this again on the big scanner, though.'

'Why?' Holly's stomach clenched in panic. Was something wrong?

Zoe squeezed her hand. 'Because the godmothers-to-be want pictures of our baby, and you can't get pictures from the portable scanner—right, Jude?'

'Absolutely,' Judith replied.

So everything was all right? And Zoe and Jude already considered the baby 'theirs'. Tears prickled at the back of

Holly's eyes. 'If you two don't stop it, I'm going to cry,' she warned.

'OK. I'll go into nag mode instead. I want you to make an appointment for all the booking-in stuff.' Judith took a urine sample container from Kieran's drawer and handed it to Holly. 'Bring a mid-stream urine sample with you. Do you want us to come with you for the booking-in scan— me as your obstetrician and Zo as your birth partner?'

'Or, if you look at it another way, both of us as your best friends,' Zoe added.

The tears won and Holly rubbed them from her cheeks. 'Thanks, but I'll be fine.'

'Feel free to change your mind.' Judith hugged her. 'Congratulations, Holls. You're going to be a mum and we're going to be—' she dropped into a very hammy Marlon Brando accent '—da godmothers.'

Zoe hugged her, too. 'Congratulations. We're so pleased.'

It was going to be all right. Judith and Zoe were going to give Holly the support she knew she wouldn't get from her family. Baby Jones wasn't going to grow up feeling deprived—he or she would have the two best 'aunties' in the world.

If only the baby's father felt the same way.

When Holly got home, late that afternoon, the first thing she saw when she opened the front door was the bunch of keys on the doormat. David certainly hadn't wasted any time. And it was clear to her now how relieved he must be. If he'd wanted her and their baby—*really* wanted them—he would have stayed and talked it through with her.

'That's it, then,' she whispered, splaying a protective hand across her abdomen. 'It's just you and me, kid. But we'll manage.' She had a good example in Tess next door,

who was a single parent. Tess was coping brilliantly and
was even finishing her degree at art college.

Though Tess had a big brother who really cared about
her, instead of a kid brother who only thought of himself.
And she had parents who were more concerned about their
daughter than about what people might say at the WI and
the Rotary Club.

'Stop feeling so sorry for yourself,' Holly said loudly.
'You've got everything you and the baby need. The best
of friends to see you through, the job of your dreams and
a house you love.'

Except the house felt too big somehow. Even when she
closed up the gaps left by David's books and CDs the
shelves didn't look right. Her clothes virtually rattled in the
wardrobe. And, despite the fact that she'd changed the
sheets twice, she was sure she could still smell David's
scent on the bed she'd shared with him. She knew that
pregnancy hormones sharpened your sense of smell, but
this was ridiculous. Even so, she ended up sleeping in her
spare room that night.

Cooking for one was too much effort, and she couldn't
handle the smells from the kitchen anyway, so she didn't
bother. The way she saw it, breakfast cereal was a good
enough meal. And at least she could keep it down. Even
the thought of plain chicken made her gag, and she couldn't
bear the idea of putting meat into her mouth.

And then it was Friday morning. Time to face David at
work, on the early shift. Holly wasn't looking forward to
it—or to the whispers that were bound to follow them
around—but she could handle the hospital grapevine. And
they were both professionals: they had a job to do and their
patients came first.

True to form, he was the first one she saw. So he hadn't

asked Sue, their consultant, to switch him to another team—or maybe he'd asked and Sue had refused.

'Morning,' she said, in as neutral a tone as she could.

'Morning.'

David's voice was equally cool and neutral. Fine. She could manage this, as long as he didn't snipe at her.

Just as she thought she'd got away with it, he added, 'You all right?'

No. My breasts are sore, I can't stop being sick and the only thing I can keep down is a bowl of cornflakes.

But then again, he didn't really want to know the answer. He was asking out of *duty*, she reminded herself, not because he cared about her. 'I'm fine,' Holly lied.

Then she remembered her manners. 'You?'

'Fine,' he said shortly.

At least he hadn't asked her the question she'd been dreading. Obviously he didn't care one way or the other. Maybe she'd just had a lucky escape. And maybe one day she'd wake up and realise it instead of yearning for him, wanting his touch.

'So is it true?' Michelle asked later, when she'd finished helping Holly deal with a severe nosebleed where the teenage boy's nose had needed cauterising.

'What?' Holly asked.

'That you and David have split up?'

'Yes. And, in answer to your next questions, yes, it's permanent and, no, I don't want to talk about it.'

'Sure.' To Holly's surprise, the nurse gave her a hug.

'What's that for?'

'Just that I've been in the same situation and I know it's tough. I couldn't handle working with my ex, so in the end I left. That's when I came here.' Michelle looked serious for a moment. 'I hope things don't go that far with you.'

'Hey. You never know, you might get a sweetness-and-light registrar in my place.'

'I prefer working with someone who tells it like it is. It means I know where I am. And I wouldn't be the only one who'd miss you. I think the whole department would be in mourning if you left.'

The lump in Holly's throat threatened to choke her and she had to swallow hard. 'I'm not planning to leave,' she said. Just to take a few months off next year. But that was a long way away.

Zoe—despite being off duty that day—met Holly during her break at half past ten, just to check she was eating properly and coping with seeing David again. And finally it was two o'clock and the end of Holly's shift. She timed it perfectly so she didn't have to face David in the rest room, and buried herself in work for her rapid response course when she got home.

The next week and a half was more of the same—cool politeness when they had to discuss a patient, and steering well clear of each other at every other time. As soon as it became obvious to everyone that there wasn't going to be a screaming row in the department, the gossip died down and it was almost as if the whole affair had never happened.

Except, Holly thought as she tried to find a spot in the rest room where she couldn't smell the hideous aroma of coffee, there was a tiny piece of physical proof. Proof which would only get bigger by the day.

Tuesday was the dampest, foggiest November morning Holly could remember, and she wasn't surprised when, halfway through her shift, Sue set the department on alert for a 'majax'—a major incident.

'There's been a multi-vehicle pile-up on the motorway,' Sue explained, 'including a coach full of ten-year-olds on a school trip. The police and ambulance service have declared a major incident. Although London City General hasn't been designated as the main hospital to receive casualties, we're pretty likely to get an influx. Holly, can you get onto the bed manager to check for vacant beds and move out as many patients as you can? Then I need you and Michelle as the triage team at the main ambulance entrance, with Siobhan fixing numbered major incident wristbands on every patient.'

Holly nodded. 'We'll make sure the triage records are accurate. Number, name and gender on any blood samples for cross-matching, yes?'

'Yes,' Sue confirmed. 'We haven't been asked for a medical incident officer but they do want a mobile medical team—David, I need you to head up the MMT working with the casualties.'

'What's the plan in the department?' Anna asked.

'Priority-one patients, with red tape, are those needing resuscitation and ventilation in Resus—that's anyone with airway or breathing problems, a GCS of twelve or less or systolic blood pressure less than 80. I'll be in there with you, Anna,' Sue explained. 'Priority-two patients, with yellow tape, are those who are less critically injured but need to be lying on a trolley—they'll be in the majors cubicles. Priority-three patients, with green tape, are the walking wounded—they'll be in the fracture clinic.' They all knew the fourth category without Sue having to tell them: white tape for patients who hadn't survived, who'd be sent to the mortuary.

'We'll set up a temporary pharmacy in the minors area, and the rest will be overflow. We need to use the major incident record folders for everybody.' The record folders were pre-prepared and numbered, containing all the necessary stationery, pre-labelled test request forms and bags for forensic evidence: they were used as standard in any major incident, because there simply wasn't time to use the computerised record system. She looked at the staff. 'Any questions?'

When everyone was silent, she nodded. 'OK, team. Let's go.'

Holly avoided David's gaze because she didn't want to answer any awkward questions. They needed as many people as possible in the emergency department and she didn't want any question marks over whether she was fit to work. She wasn't going anywhere near X-Ray so she should be absolutely fine. As for her weak stomach, she'd be much too busy to even think about nausea.

With the help of the bed manager, she cleared as many patients as she could from the department. And then the paramedics started bringing the cases through. She and Michelle worked methodically together to assess each patient, giving each one a cruciform card and sticking coloured tape on them, while Siobhan the receptionist filled in the records and put a matching number on the major incident wristband around each patient's wrist.

One woman came in, very agitated and wanting to leave straight away. 'I'm fine—don't worry about me. But what about my children? I need to know they're all right,' she said.

'We'll check you over first, and then you can talk to the relatives' liaison team,' Holly said. 'May I examine you?'

'I need to find out about my children.'

'The quicker I can examine you, the quicker you'll be able to see the liaison team,' Holly said gently. 'I know you're worried, but you wouldn't be here if the paramedics weren't concerned about you.'

As soon as Holly saw the abrasions from the lap belt, she was on full alert: the injury pattern could mean blunt abdominal trauma. Lap-belt marks were associated with rupture of the small intestine. 'Were you a passenger?'

'Yes.'

Holly went through the 'ample' mnemonic—allergies, medication, past medical history, last meal, events leading up to her admission—and Siobhan took the notes. 'Any tenderness here?' she asked, palpating the woman's abdomen.

'A little bit.'

Holly definitely didn't like the fullness or the slightly doughy feeling of the woman's abdomen: from experience, she knew that it meant a bleed inside the abdomen. 'Miche, we need bloods—cross-match and gases.' Because she was on triage, she wouldn't have time to do an ultrasound scan or a diagnostic peritoneal lavage, but she assigned her patient to a senior nurse and a doctor who could perform the procedure. 'Your injuries might be a bit more than you think, but we'll get you sorted as soon as we can, and then we'll find out about your children,' she reassured the patient.

Her next case was a traumatic pneumothorax, where gas had collected in the space around the lungs and caused the lungs to collapse; the patient was gasping for breath and clutching at his chest as if he was in pain. There was a blue tinge around his lips and as soon as Holly listened to his chest she couldn't hear any sounds on one side. Holly knew they were already stretched in Resus, so she had no choice. If she didn't act now, their patient could die.

'I'm going to give you oxygen to help you breathe,' she said, putting the oxygen mask on their patient.

'Needle thoracotomy, Miche,' she said.

The nurse nodded. 'I'll prepare the site,' she said, and swabbed the area.

'This is going to hurt a little bit, sweetheart,' Holly said to her patient, 'but it's going to help you breathe a lot more easily, then we can check you over.'

As soon as Michelle gave her the angiocath, Holly inserted it into the space over the top of the rib and listened for the rush of air. 'Definitely a pneumothorax,' she said. She removed the needle, secured the angiocath, then prepared to insert a chest tube.

'Priority one,' she told Siobhan. 'Get him checked over in Resus and then admitted—he'll need a chest X-ray to check the placement of the tube, and the tube will need to be in for at least twenty-four hours to keep air out of the pleural cavity.' If the lung hadn't reinflated within five days, the patient might need surgery.

Before her next patient arrived, one of the nurses who'd been on a break came over, her face white. 'There's been a problem at the scene,' she said. 'I saw it on the news. They were trying to get the kids out of the bus and something went wrong—some of the rescue workers have been hurt.'

David.

Holly tried to keep her voice calm. 'Did they say who? Any of our lot?'

'No—it's a bit of a mess out there. Nobody's sure what's going on.'

It would be just like David to go in and help, with no thought for his own safety. Supposing he was hurt? And if he was trapped under something heavy he might have severe crush injuries. If he was bleeding heavily and nobody could reach him to staunch the flow and put in a line to get fluid replacement into him, he could go into hypovolaemic shock—meaning that his blood wouldn't circulate properly and his organs would start to fail. He could even bleed to death.

Supposing he was *dead*?

Suddenly, Holly found her hands were shaking. Her whole body felt chilled, almost in a kind of stupor. Was it true that she'd never see him again? Never see those beautiful cornflower-blue eyes crinkling at the corners as he shared a joke? Never see the sensual curve of his mouth? Never feel his arms curved round her as he slept, or the warmth of his breath against her skin?

Please, God, no. I know I said I hated him, but I didn't mean it. I didn't want anything to happen to him. Please, don't let him be dead, she begged silently. Please, let him be all right.

'Holls, you look all in,' Michelle said, touching her gently on the shoulder. 'You're due a break.'

'You both are,' Lesley Black, one of the registrars on another emergency team, informed them. 'Sue told me to come and kick you out for twenty minutes or so.'

'And who's going to make sure *she* takes a break?' Holly asked.

Lesley grinned. 'That would be you, Holls. You're the only one who's scary enough to get away with it—but wait till you've had your own break, OK?'

'OK. Thanks, Lesley. Come on, Miche. I need a drink.' Just water and a sit-down would do.

But she couldn't stop thinking about David. Had he been involved in the accident? Was he all right?

He couldn't be hurt. He couldn't be dead. He *couldn't* be. He had to live—for her sake. For their unborn child's sake.

So what if he didn't really love her? She had enough love for two. She could make it work. She'd tell him she was keeping the baby, ask him to be part of their lives. Even if it was just an odd corner, it would be enough.

Just, please, keep him safe until I can tell him, she prayed. Please, don't let him have been hurt.

CHAPTER TWELVE

DAVID couldn't remember ever being this cold. The chill from the fog had seeped into his bones, and even though he'd been frantically busy with patients since the moment he'd stepped out of the car it wasn't enough to keep him warm.

He was so used to working in the emergency department in a hospital that he'd forgotten what it was like to be in the middle of a major incident. Noise everywhere—the moans from the injured, the static on the radio communications from the fire, police and ambulance services, sirens blaring as another ambulance ferried a load back to the hospital, the swish of cars and rumble of lorries passing on the wet road on the other side of the motorway. People screaming in panic. Frightened children sobbing. Commands being barked at the medical teams—was that his own voice doing all that yelling? Flashing lights and luminous jackets wherever he looked. And the smell: fresh blood that had seeped into the puddles around them. He could almost taste the sharp metallic tang in the air.

'OK, love.' He soothed a woman who was trapped in the driver's seat of her car. 'We'll get you out as soon as we can.' Though when he shone his flashlight into the car it didn't look good. The car had crumpled and he couldn't see her legs. He'd need the fire service to cut her out before he could move her—and they'd need to be very careful. If her legs were crushed, the weight of the metal around her could be the only thing keeping the blood in her body. The second she was moved, she could suffer catastrophic blood loss. Even if she was spared that, there was a danger of renal failure due to the circulation problems.

Then she whispered something that sent his whole body into a tailspin.

'My baby.'

'In the back?' he asked, shining the flashlight into the back. He couldn't see an infant car seat.

'No.' The word was more of a sob.

Her hand was splayed across her abdomen and he realised what she meant.

'How many weeks are you?' he asked gently.

'Eleven.'

The same as Holly—if she hadn't already had the termination.

Holly.

The word was like a knife twisting in his gut. He couldn't think about her now. Not when all hell was let loose around him. He had to concentrate on his patients. David blinked hard to focus himself. 'I'm going to get the fire crew to stabilise the car, then we'll get you out,' he promised.

Once the fire crew had put chocks under the car to stop unexpected movements and had disconnected the ignition, it was safe for David to check her airway. Her breathing was fine but he really wanted to get a spinal board under her. It was impossible the way the car was at the moment. 'I need someone to support my patient's neck—' if her cervical spine wasn't stable and her neck wasn't held completely still she could end up paralysed '—and we need to cut her out,' he told the fire crew quietly. 'I'm not sure how badly her legs are damaged, so we'll need to move her onto a board and out of here very fast. And she's pregnant.'

'We'll start stabilising the car now.'

David knew how frightened his patient must be—as well

as her injuries from the accident she was panicking about her baby, she was in a claustrophobic situation, with green plastic sheets surrounding her in the tiny space while the fire crew made the glass in the car safe and cut through the pillars, and someone was holding her head tightly. He kept talking to her, reassuring her, checking her pulse as best as he could—it was in the normal range, but the weight of the car could be keeping her blood pressure up. He pressed her finger and mentally said, 'Capillary return,' as he watched the skin closely: to his relief, the blanching caused by the pressure of his finger had returned to normal before he'd even got to 'return'. That was a good sign, but his patient was anxious and sweaty—possibly grade-two hypovolaemia, meaning that she'd lost up to thirty per cent of her blood and was in danger of going into shock. He needed to know where the bleeding was coming from: a miscarriage or a crush injury?

Once the roof of the car was off, David was in a better position to put in a Haemaccel drip to help prevent shock. Quickly, he and the paramedic who'd been supporting her head inserted the spinal board behind the patient. The fire crew supported her weight on the board while they reclined her seat.

'Her legs are caught,' David said quietly.

The fire crew did a 'dashboard roll', using hydraulic equipment to pull the dashboard far enough forward to lift her out. Together, they slid her up the spinal board, and David noticed the signs he'd hoped not to see: his patient was definitely miscarrying. He wanted her lower legs checked properly to make sure there weren't any crush injuries. He was particularly worried about compartment syndrome, sometimes caused by the legs being trapped, where increased muscle compartment pressure obstructed the blood flow, the muscles became filled with fluid and the pressure increased, and a vicious cycle was set up where the higher the pressure, the lower the blood flow.

'My baby?' she said again. 'I feel wet. Between my legs. Please, it isn't my baby, is it? Please?'

'I'm sorry,' he said, holding her hand. 'I'm so sorry. But we'll get you to hospital now for treatment.'

She said nothing, simply closed her eyes, her misery too deep for tears, and David wished he could wave a magic wand and make it all right for her. Make it so the accident had never happened.

Poor woman.

Unbidden, Holly filled his mind. She'd miscarried, too. Just before her first A-level exam. Had it been like this for her? Lonely and frightened as the bleeding started and the little life seeped from her body…

He shook himself. If he didn't block his emotions right now he wouldn't be able to do his job properly. There were people out here who needed his help. He owed it to them to give them his full concentration. To save their lives. It was who he was, what he did.

Besides, Holly had already made it clear she didn't want him in her life any more.

The paramedic put foam pads on each side of their patient's head and strapped her to the board to secure her cervical spine. David helped to carry her to the ambulance, explained his concerns to the paramedics and gave instructions to be relayed back to base, then went on to his next patient. Before he could get there, he heard one of the team yelling to him.

'David—I need you here! Now!'

'What's the problem?' he asked.

'I can't get my patient's airway clear or put a tube down.' Intubation was usually done when the patient didn't have a gag reflex or couldn't breathe properly due to trauma or blockage. It helped the patient's breathing and protected the airway against blood and vomit.

There wasn't enough time to do an emergency tracheostomy. 'I'll do a needle cricothyrotomy,' David said. 'I need a 12G cannula-over-needle attached to a syringe, oxygen and tubing.'

He palpated the patient's neck to find the cricothyroid membrane, then passed the needle and cannula through the membrane into the trachea. Aspiration of air confirmed that he was in to the trachea. Slowly, he pushed the cannula into position and withdrew the needle. He connected the cannula to oxygen tubing with a side hole. 'Keep it at fifteen litres a minute,' he said. 'Cover the side hole with your thumb for one second in five to give the patient jets of oxygen—he should be able to exhale partially in the four seconds between jets, but he won't be able to get rid of all the carbon dioxide when he breathes out so it's only a holding measure. He needs to go to Resus *now*.'

Fractures, a possible spinal injury and a haemothorax—where blood had collected in the pleural cavity and David needed to insert a chest drain to get rid of the fluid, as well as adding intravenous fluids to stop the patient going into hypovolaemic shock from loss of blood—followed in quick succession.

'You need a break. Take ten, have some tea with sugar in it,' said the paramedic when David had stabilised the patient with the haemothorax. 'You haven't stopped since you got here.' When David started to protest, the paramedic added, 'If you keep going at this rate you'll collapse and be no use to us. Take ten, for our sake if not your own.'

'Yeah, you're right. Thanks.' The hot sweet tea they gave him at the temporary base tasted revolting, but it was enough to revive him.

Though taking a break also meant he had time to think

again. Time to think about his patient with the miscarriage, and Holly. He hadn't been there for Holly twelve years ago when she'd lost their baby; this time he'd let her down again. Stormed off, thought of himself before thinking of her. He knew Holly could be difficult and stubborn, pig-headed in the extreme. So when she'd snapped at him, why hadn't he just backed off? Gone for a walk or something and come back with flowers and a hug? Why hadn't he told her that he wasn't going to leave her, that she'd just have to put up with him, and when she'd had time to get used to the idea that they were going to have a baby he'd be there to support her all the way?

But no. He'd pushed her. And she'd reacted to the pressure by saying she was going to have a termination.

Or had she? He racked his brains. Had she actually *said* she was going to have a termination? Or had she been trying to point out, in typical in-your-face-shock Holly fashion, that she needed time to get used to the idea of being pregnant before she could discuss what happened next?

Since she'd asked him to move out they'd barely spoken on the ward, except when they were forced to discuss a case. So he had no idea how she was or what her plans were or whether she'd had the termination—or even if she'd ever have anything to do with him again. But the look on his patient's face haunted him. Supposing it had been Holly in that car, losing their baby?

The thought was unbearable.

And that was when David realised how much he still loved Holly. He always had and he always would. But whenever things went wrong they'd been too quick to judge each other, and judge each other unfairly. How was he ever going to get this mess sorted out?

'I have to know,' he heard a voice saying on the radio, between static.

Holly's voice? No. Of course not. Wishful thinking—or maybe hallucinations brought on by the nightmare of this place, wanting to hear the sound of someone familiar to comfort him.

'Is David all right?'

That got his attention fully. He probably wasn't the only David out here, but…it sounded so like Holly, with the edges rubbed off her once-posh accent. *Could* it be her? Hope made his pulse thud hard.

'David who?' the radio operator asked.

'David Neave.'

David's heart almost stopped. It *was* her.

'On the news it said some of the rescue team was injured. Was he…?' Her voice caught. 'Was he one of them?'

'I dunno, love. I can try and get a message out to the teams, if you like.'

Holly was asking about him? She was worried about him? She still cared? By the time it had sunk in and David had gone over to the radio operator to try to talk to Holly himself it was too late. Holly was gone. She was probably back in the thick of things in the emergency department, dealing with triage.

'Are you all right, mate? You look as if you've seen a ghost.'

'Must be something they put in the tea,' David said, forcing himself to sound light-hearted. 'Were you talking to Holly Jones at London City General just now?'

'Yeah.' The radio operator frowned. 'Are you the bloke she was asking about, by any chance?'

David nodded. 'Can you get through to her again?'

'Doubt it, mate. But I can ask someone to pass a message on to her, if you like.'

'Yes, please. Tell her I'm all right.' Tell her I've been stupid and I love her and I need a second chance—no, a third chance, he corrected himself. Tell her I want to make a family with her.

No. He wanted to tell her face to face. So there'd be no mistakes this time. 'Tell her I'll see her soon.'

'OK, mate.'

And then David was back on the front line again, triaging patients. Raging with the paramedics at the stupidity of parents who didn't keep their children strapped securely into child seats when they couldn't save a child who'd been catapulted straight through the windscreen. Assessing head injuries, dealing with a suspected partial aortic rupture—common in high-energy impacts such as the one they were dealing with, and David privately didn't hold out much hope for the patient—and more fractures.

Finally his team was relieved. David didn't care that he was dirty, sweaty, smelly and covered in blood. He needed to see Holly. If she wasn't in the emergency department, he'd try her house. But he needed to see her. To talk to her. To ask her to give him another chance.

He walked through the main ambulance entrance. That was where Sue had posted her, so it was the most likely place he'd find her. But he couldn't see her anywhere.

'Is Holly around?' he asked one of the nurses.

'Somewhere, yes. I haven't seen her for a while, though.'

'Thanks.' Well, he'd keep looking until he found her.

He had to ask three more people before he discovered what had happened.

'There was an accident about an hour ago—someone caught her with a trolley. Then she said she didn't feel very well. I'm not sure if she's gone home.'

'Thanks.' David strode out to a safe area where he could use his mobile phone, and rang Holly. The phone rang once, twice, and her answering machine kicked in. He drummed his fingers as he waited for the short message to end. Pick up. *Pick up,* he urged silently. At the beep, he spoke rapidly. 'Hol, it's me. David. Are you OK? I heard about the accident. If you're there, pick up, please. Hol?'

No answer.

Even *she* wouldn't be that stubborn, would she?

He tried her mobile, but that was switched off.

He tried her home phone again: still no answer. So either she was out or she didn't want to talk to him or… He nearly doubled over as a nasty thought occurred to him. Holly had been in an accident. She hadn't felt well. He'd been wrong about her in the past, so he'd probably made a wrong assumption about the termination—which meant there was a chance she was miscarrying. Just like the woman out there in the pile-up.

He switched off his mobile, went back into the hospital and dialled Judith's extension.

'Hello, Maternity. Judith Bailey's phone.'

'Can I speak to Judith, please?'

'Sorry, she's with a patient. Can anyone else help?'

He hoped his voice wasn't shaking as much as his hand was. 'It's David Neave from Emergency. Is she with Holly Jones?'

'I'm sorry, I can't discuss patients with anyone apart from relatives.'

Which had to mean yes—otherwise the midwife would have said no, wouldn't she?

Holly was in Maternity. Which meant she could be losing their baby. Which meant he had to be with her. Now. 'Thank you,' he said, and replaced the receiver.

CHAPTER THIRTEEN

DAVID didn't bother waiting for the lifts. He ran up the stairs three at a time and headed straight for the midwives' desk, ignoring the strange looks from patients and relatives. 'Lulu, which room is she in? Please?' he asked the senior midwife, who was writing up notes.

'Who?'

'Holly.' He only just managed to keep his voice under control.

Louise frowned. 'Are you all right, David?'

Of course he wasn't all right! The love of his life was losing their baby, and if he didn't get to see her right now and be by her side he'd go crazy. Then he realised why Louise was looking at him so oddly.

'There was a pile-up on the motorway. I was on the mobile medical team and I've just got back to the hospital. I haven't had a chance to clean myself up yet,' he said. 'Actually, you've probably got one of my patients here— she was caught up in the middle of it and had a miscarriage. I've just heard about Holly, and—'

'I'm sorry, David,' Louise cut in. 'You know the rules about patient confidentiality. I can't give information to anyone who isn't a relative.'

Oh, for goodness' sake! Couldn't the rules be bent just for once? Louise knew perfectly well who he was—she knew he wasn't a nutter or a stalker or... He took a shuddering breath, trying to calm himself down. The midwife was only doing her job and following protocols. And for all she knew he could be temporarily unhinged by the mess he'd been helping to clear up.

Maybe he *was* temporarily unhinged—by worry about Holly. He'd jabbered away at Louise and had barely let her get a word in edgeways. No doubt his eyes were wild and staring and his hair was sticking up. He already knew he was filthy and his clothes were soaked.

But he needed to be with Holly. She was more important than any protocols.

'I *am* a relative,' he said quietly. 'It's my baby.'

Louise sucked in a breath. 'Then this has to be Holly's call.'

'Ask her. Please. Or let me talk to Jude. Hol *is* with Jude, isn't she?' He raked a hand through his hair. 'I know you have to follow the rules, Lulu, but I wouldn't ask if it wasn't life or death. If she's losing our baby I need to be with her. I've been an idiot and she's furious with me, and you know how bloody-minded Hol can be so she'll probably say she doesn't want to talk to me. But I love her, Lulu. She's the only thing that means anything in my life. It's taken me long enough to realise it. I—' His voice cracked. 'I love her. Please. Please, let me see her.'

'Stay here, and I'll ask.'

David shook his head. 'I can't stay here. I swear, I won't burst into the room or cause any trouble. But I need to know how she is.'

Louise relented. 'As long as you promise to stay outside until she says she'll talk to you.'

'I promise. Thank you,' he said humbly, and followed her over to one of the small side-rooms.

Oh, God. Holly was in a side-room, not the ward. Which meant she'd probably lost their baby. The same thing all over again—she'd needed him and he'd let her down. He hadn't been there.

The seconds ticked by, slower and slower, as if some unseen resistance was pushing the second hand backwards.

If only it could.

If he could turn back time it could all be different. Starting from when they were eighteen. Or if he could only turn it back a little while, he'd turn it back to that last row. He'd change everything. He'd lay his heart open to Holly and show her he trusted her, that she could trust him, too. He'd tell her how much he loved her.

The door opened. Lulu came out, followed by Judith.

'Jude! How is she?' he asked urgently.

'She needs to rest. I don't want her upset,' Judith warned.

'I swear, I won't upset her. I just need to know she's all right. That our…' His throat refused to work any more. To his horror, the word he'd meant to say came out as a sob.

Judith looked torn between protecting Holly and comforting him. 'As her doctor, I really shouldn't let you in there.'

David drew in a shuddering breath. 'And as her best friend?' he asked quietly.

'As her best friend I should be planting my fist right on your nose. Or somewhere that hurts a lot more.'

'She's stubborn and I'm stupid. It's not the best combination. But I love her, Jude. And I need to see her.' He swallowed hard. 'She was asking for me earlier.'

Judith frowned. 'I've been with her since the second she came up here. She's done no such thing.'

'Before. When I was out at the crash scene. Some of the rescue workers were hurt, and I heard her ask the radio operator if I was OK. But by the time I realised it was her, she'd already gone so I couldn't talk to her.' David felt as if he was hyperventilating. He couldn't get enough air into his lungs and he felt panicky and light-headed. *When would they let him see Holly?* 'I tried to get a message to her.'

Judith folded her arms. 'You're right. She's stubborn and you're stupid. I'll be waiting right here, listening. And if I hear even the slightest rise in your voice, you'll be out of my ward faster than the speed of light,' she informed him, a note of steel in her voice.

'I promise I'll whisper,' David said hoarsely, almost sagging in relief. At last. They were going to let him see her.

And then he was at Holly's bedside, holding her hand tightly in his.

'David, I've got a drip in. That hurts,' she said softly.

'Sorry.' He'd been so desperate to hold her that he hadn't even noticed the cannula in her hand and the IV running down. He'd just needed the contact, skin to skin. He released her hand and squeezed the other one instead. 'Are you OK?'

'Yeah. I think so.' She raised an eyebrow. 'You look like hell.'

'I feel it. I came back to the department to see you and they told me about the accident. I'm sorry, I know I'm grubby and I probably smell, but I couldn't stop to shower or anything—I had to know if you were all right.'

'I just got knocked over by a trolley. It was my own fault. I was in the way. Nothing serious. But then I felt a bit funny. When I went to the loo, I realised I'd started spotting.' She took a shuddering breath. 'I promised Jude I'd tell her if I was worried about anything at all, so I came up here to get it checked out.'

'Oh, Hol.' He could hardly see her for the tears in his eyes, tears he tried to blink back. But he was running on empty now. He was so tired and he just couldn't keep his emotions compartmentalised, the way a doctor was trained to do. Not any more. 'I'm so sorry. I screwed up. But if you can forgive me, I swear I'll never let you down again. I love you, Hol. I love you more than anything. I've been stupid and proud and panicky and...' His voice faded as he realised that she was crying. 'Don't cry,' he said, brushing a tear from her face and leaving a smudge of dirt across her cheek. 'Everything's going to be all right. I promise.'

'I thought you were hurt,' she whispered. 'That you were one of the rescue workers who'd been—' She choked the word off. 'I thought I'd never see you again and it was too late.'

'I know. I was there when you came through on the radio. But I wasn't taking things in—when I realised it was you, it was too late. You'd already gone. I tried to get a message through to you that I was still alive and kicking and sorting out my patients.'

'I didn't get it. We were busy. Well, you know that. You were there on the front line.'

'Yeah.'

'You're covered in blood and I don't know what else.'

He looked down at the dirty smudges on her sheets. 'I'll launder your sheets myself. By hand, if I have to.'

She smiled through her tears. 'You're crazy.'

'About you, yes. I always have been, always will be.'

'Me, too.'

'Say it,' he begged. 'Just say it.' He needed to hear her say it. Needed to know she meant it. 'Please?'

'I love you.' There were tears in her eyes, too. 'And I'm sorry I went off at the deep end. I said a lot of things I didn't mean.'

He sighed. 'Me, too.'

'You were right. It was my hormones talking.'

He shook his head. 'It wasn't all you. I'm sorry I pressured you. I panicked you into saying something that...' He swallowed hard. How could he bring up what she'd said now that she'd just lost their baby? 'I'm sorry,' he whispered.

'I didn't have a termination, David. I couldn't.'

'I know.' But he had to be honest with her. No more misunderstandings. 'I persuaded myself that your ambition would come first and a baby would be in the way. But then I had a patient today who lost her baby. It made me think about you, think properly—and then I realised I'd steamrollered you, so you only said it to shut me up.'

She nodded. 'I'm so, so sorry.'

'Hey. Don't blame yourself.' It wasn't her fault she'd miscarried again. If anything, it was his fault. He'd put too much stress on her at a time when she'd needed nurturing. And he should have told Sue about the pregnancy, in confidence, to make sure that Holly wasn't overworked in the department. 'Next time,' he said softly, 'I'll be there right from the moment you do the pregnancy test. We'll watch the line turn blue together. And we'll have the most beautiful baby in the world.'

'Not for at least another two years.'

He nodded. She'd just lost their child. Again. Of course she'd be wary of trying again. He wouldn't rush her. 'No pressure. We'll wait for however long it takes until you're well again and you feel ready to try.'

Holly smiled. 'Actually, make that more like three years. I'd rather this one was out of nappies first.'

David's head was spinning. Either his blood sugar was low or he was hallucinating. 'What?'

'Most babies are out of nappies between the ages of two and three. So we're not going to try for a second baby until this one—' she rubbed her tummy '—is at least two.'

A *second* baby? He stared at her. 'You mean...our baby's all right?'

'Yes.' She frowned. 'But you knew that. Jude's only keeping me here for observation because we're really busy downstairs and she doesn't trust me not to go and finish my shift.'

He shook his head. 'Nobody would tell me *anything*. Patient confidentiality.'

She tightened her fingers round his. 'Jude did a scan and everything's fine. The bleeding's stopped now.'

So they really were going to have a baby? Everything really was going to be all right? 'Oh, Hol.' He wrapped his arms around her and squeezed so tightly that she squeaked. Judith rushed straight in.

'David, Holly's supposed to be *resting*!'

'Sorry, sorry, sorry.' He held his hands up in surrender. 'Don't chuck me out. Please. It's just… Now I know the baby's OK, I just…' He shook his head. 'Sorry. I'm not making a lot of sense.'

'Holly's going to be absolutely fine. You know how common spotting is in the first trimester. It doesn't mean she's going to have a miscarriage. Though I want her on bed-rest for the next couple of days, and *no* excitement.' Judith narrowed her eyes. 'Understand?'

'Yes— No.' He couldn't take it in.

'Jude, don't bully the poor man. He's been on the mobile medical team for hours without a proper break or any refreshment, knowing him,' Holly said.

'Says the woman who was doing exactly the same thing in the emergency department downstairs,' David rebuked her.

'No cotton wool,' Holly warned.

'Whatever you say, boss.' He looked at Judith. 'The baby's definitely OK?'

Judith sighed. 'You're not going to be happy until you see the ultrasound, are you?'

'No, he's not,' Holly said.

Judith rolled her eyes. 'OK, Holls, you know the drill.

Lie back and relax.' She put gel on Holly's abdomen, then ran the scanner head over it.

'That's our baby?' David asked in hushed awe as the picture came up on the screen. He reached out towards the screen, his hand shaking.

'Not much bigger than a tadpole at the moment—but, yes, that's our baby,' Holly said.

'Oh, wow.'

'We've got a photograph. Jude did me one last week. It's in my handbag. We could, um, photocopy it and enlarge it. If you want to pin it on the board in your office, that is.'

He could feel the smile spreading over his face. The hours he'd spent in the fog and drizzle just melted away. He was going to be a father. He and Holly were going to be parents. And she was happy to go public about it. 'Our baby,' he said softly.

'You do realise this baby's going to be terribly spoiled because his father will never be able to say the word "no",' Judith teased. 'David's got that besotted look already.'

'I'm besotted all right. With my baby—and its mother.'

'His,' Judith corrected.

He stared at her. 'I didn't think you could tell this early.'

'Jude calls all babies "he",' Holly explained.

'Sounds better than "it",' Judith defended herself.

David squeezed Holly's hand. 'Agreed. Though I don't mind if we have a girl or a boy. Jude, would you mind giving us some time, please?'

'Sure.' Judith switched off the scanner and handed Holly some paper towels.

'I'll do that,' David said, and tenderly wiped the gel from her abdomen. When Jude had left them alone again, he took her hand. 'Holly, I know we've had our differences, but I love you—and I want to bring the baby up with you.' He paused. 'I want to live with you again. Preferably as your husband, but if you'd rather do it without a piece of paper that's fine by me, too. Just as long as we're together.'

'You're not just saying that out of duty?'

He frowned. Why on earth would she think he wanted to stay with her out of *duty*? 'Of course not. I'm saying it because I love you, and I want to spend the rest of my life with you—*and* our baby. Babies,' he corrected.

Relief spread over her face and for a moment he thought she was going to cry, but then she lifted her chin and was back to the imperious Holly he'd known and loved for years. 'If you wrap me in cotton wool and fuss and steam-roller me, you can expect trouble,' she informed him.

'You're stubborn and I'm stupid. So I guess that means I'll try to do what I think's the right thing when it's nothing of the sort, you'll throw hissy fits, I'll ignore them and we'll rub along fine,' David said.

She laughed. 'Yeah, you're probably right.'

'Life with you is never going to be dull. Even outside the emergency department,' he said.

'It's going to get very lively shortly,' she said thoughtfully.

He frowned. 'How do you mean?'

'We're going to have to go to Liverpool—'

'And face our mums,' he finished. 'Ah.'

'I'm a match for my mother now,' Holly said.

'And I'm a match for mine. No problems there, then.' He grinned. 'So, are you going to marry me?'

'Jude said no excitement. Weddings are exciting.'

'No excitement. Hmm. You definitely won't want to see my new flat, then.'

'Why?'

'Put it this way, the décor of my last place was tame compared to this one.'

'And you're going to have to face that after the day from hell?' She pulled a face. 'I'll do you a deal. Spring me from here and we can go home together. As in *home* home.'

'If I spring you—and I mean *if*—you have to stay in bed for the next couple of days,' David warned.

'Uh-huh.'

'Why don't I believe you?' He sighed. 'Sue's going to have to know one way or another. Either you stay in here on bed-rest for a couple of days, or I'll take a couple of days off and you'll be at home on bed-rest for a couple of days with me keeping an eye on you. Your choice.'

'I'll go bananas if I have to stay in bed.'

'On the other hand, I could suggest your mum come and look after you…'

Holly gave him a disgusted look. 'That's blackmail.'

'Tactics. If it worked for the treadmill, it'll work for our baby.'

'Oh, no. You're going to plot with Jude and Zo, aren't you?'

He gave her a wicked smile. 'And Tess. I know I won't be able to do it on my own, so I'm calling in reinforcements.'

'I give in. Spring me, and I swear I'll do whatever you say for the next two days.'

'Now, that,' David said with a grin, 'is full of possibilities…'

CHAPTER FOURTEEN

DAVID brought Holly a tray of cornflakes and a glass of still water. 'Lunch is served.'

'Thanks, but you really don't have to do this. I'm perfectly capable of getting up and having lunch downstairs.'

'And then you'll start working, or you'll be tempted by the treadmill, or your nesting instinct will kick in and you'll decide you need to clean out all the kitchen cupboards.' He folded his arms. 'Tough. Jude said bed-rest, and bed-rest it is.'

'Right.' She sighed and toyed with her cornflakes.

'Don't even think about going on hunger strike,' he warned.

'I'm not. But I'm just not programmed to be *still*.'

'True.' David stripped off his sweater and jeans.

'What are you doing?'

He slid into bed beside her. 'Keeping you company to stop you being bored. Hol, I know you hate staying put, but it's for the baby's sake.'

'I know. And I'm trying not to moan.' At his sceptical look, she glowered. 'Really I am.'

He shifted so that she was lying in his arms with her head on his shoulder. 'Sue doesn't want you doing Friday or Saturday night this week. So either you do two half-days—that's afternoons—or you stay at home. Not on bed-rest,' he added, when Holly started to protest, 'but on a promise that you're not going to do anything remotely strenuous.'

175

'When did you get this bossy? You've been taking lessons from my mother,' she grumbled.

'Now, that's a good idea,' he teased. He dropped a kiss on her hair. 'So are we going to get married, Hol?'

'Is that a proposal?'

'No, it's a question.' He held her closer. 'When I propose, I'll do it properly. But I'm not going to propose unless I know the answer.'

Holly was surprised. 'Do you *really* not know what I'll say?'

'No, because I'm never going to take you for granted.'

She smiled. 'I'll hold that thought.' She sighed. 'But I don't want a wedding where my mother will take over. Would you mind if we had a civil do?'

'Anything you want, as long as you spend the rest of your life with me.' He stroked her abdomen. 'So it is going to be a yes?'

'You'll have to ask me,' Holly said, with a wicked grin.

The following Monday, when they were both off duty, David took her to the London Aquarium again for a wander around the sharks. 'Happy anniversary, Hol. Well, weekiversary.'

'Three months ago we came here and agreed to take it slowly. And now we're going to be a family. It doesn't seem real, almost,' Holly said.

'I could prove that it's true. But then we might get thrown out.' He grinned. 'And if you want to hold our wedding reception here, it could be a bit embarrassing.'

Holly's heart started to beat faster. Was David intending to propose on one knee right here, right now? Here, to make it third time lucky?

But he strolled on to the next display. They passed the rays and the terrapins—and although he insisted on taking another look at the sharks, he didn't say what she was half expecting to hear.

When they left the aquarium, she realised that he probably *wasn't* intending to propose today. And she was shocked to find that she was actually disappointed.

Maybe she should propose to him…

'What's up?' David asked as they walked back to the tube station.

'Nothing.' She paused. 'Where are we going next?'

'Playing tourist.' He wouldn't tell her anything more than that.

Holly curbed her impatience, but when they left the tube at Tower Bridge she scoffed. 'We could have walked here from the aquarium. It isn't exactly a long way.'

'I know. But it's the first week of December, it's cold and I don't want you…' He stopped to correct himself. 'I don't want to overdo things in my condition.'

Holly chuckled. 'Don't you mean *my* condition?'

'Yes, but you hate being mollycoddled, so I'm trying to do it without annoying you.' He took her hand and they climbed the stairs to the walkway overlooking the Thames. It was almost deserted, the tourists either preferring warmer, indoor attractions or tempted by the Christmas displays in Oxford Street.

A few flakes of snow drifted on the wind and Holly leaned against the railing, enjoying the view over the river. 'This is spectacular,' she said.

'Holly Jones.'

The fact he'd said her full name—as well as the odd tone—alerted her. She looked at David to discover that he'd dropped to one knee beside her.

He took her left hand and raised it to his lips. 'You're the love of my life. You always have been and always will be. Will you marry me?'

There was a lump in her throat the size of a yacht, but she managed to whisper, 'Yes.'

He kissed her ring finger and stood up. 'Good. After lunch, we're going shopping for an engagement ring. Together.'

She couldn't speak.

'Are you crying?' he asked, brushing away the moisture from her face.

'Melting snow,' she lied.

He held her tightly. 'I love you, Holly. Prickles and all. Now, let's get out of the cold.'

In the gift shop, David bought her a snow globe containing a tiny model of Tower Bridge. 'Just to remind you of a certain question,' he said.

'Even including the snow.' She smiled back at him, then caught his arm. 'Look.'

He read the notice and his eyes widened. 'We can get married in exactly the same place I proposed to you? Wow.' He smiled. 'I think it's fate, Hol.'

'Me, too.' She grinned. 'My poor mother. She's going to get three shocks next week.'

'Three nice surprises,' David corrected.

The following weekend, David drove them up to Liverpool. They'd booked a table at a new, very swanky restaurant, and now it was time for them to lay all the demons of the past to rest.

'Are you ready for this?' David asked as they reached the restaurant.

Holly took a deep breath. 'Yes. I know Mum's going to be difficult about this, but I'm a big girl now, and she'll just have to accept our choices.' She glanced at David. 'How about you?'

'Snap. Well, except obviously I'm not a girl.'

The joke was so poor Holly knew that David was as nervous as she was. But they'd both agreed that they couldn't tell their parents on the phone: this was something that had to be done face to face. They'd also agreed that a public place would mean less chance of fireworks: Laura might be bossy, but she also didn't create scenes in public. Not when it might involve gossip and her family's good name at least.

David spoke to the waiter and found their table. 'I asked if we could be as far away from the kitchen as possible. Are you OK, or do you want me to ask for a different table?' he asked as he held Holly's chair for her.

'I'm OK, thanks. Just cross your fingers that nobody near us orders garlic.'

'I'll get you some water.' He stroked her cheek. 'Don't look so worried. Telling them isn't going to be that bad.'

'It was last time. Well, for me,' she amended.

Holly, how could you be so stupid? She could still hear it, even now. And Holly had a nasty feeling they'd be the first words out of Laura's mouth this time, too.

As if he could read her mind, David said softly, 'This time it's different. I know before your mother does. If she's going to have a fight with anyone, it'll be me, not you.'

Holly lifted her chin. 'I can look after myself.'

'I know. But after that scare I don't want anything upsetting you.'

'I'll be fine. Drop the cotton wool.'

'Isn't that my cue to stick my fingers in my ears and say, "La, la, la, I can't hear you"?' He kissed the tip of her nose. 'I'll get you that water. Still, with plenty of ice and a slice of lime?'

She nodded. 'Thank you.'

'Just don't crunch all the ice cubes before we've told them, or they'll realise you're having a craving and work it out for themselves.' He winked, and went to order her drink.

Holly sat at the table, twisting her fingers and wishing she'd gone with him. Despite her bravado, it still worried her. She was going to tell her mother that she was pregnant. And seeing the man who'd ruined her dreams twelve years ago. And not getting married in the parish church near the Jones's house. Laura Jones wasn't going to take it well.

'Holly, there you are.' Laura bustled over to the table, kissed her daughter's cheek and sat opposite her. 'Your father's parking the car. I still don't know why you insisted on meeting us here when there's a perfectly good— Oh.' She stopped in midflow when David returned with Holly's drink.

'You remember David Neave, don't you, Mum?' Holly asked.

'Ye-es.' Laura looked faintly uncomfortable. 'Hello, David. How are you?'

'Fine, thank you, Mrs Jones.'

Laura clearly registered the change in his accent, and Holly pressed her foot against David's as he sat down beside her. She didn't care if her mother was a snob. David was her choice and it was staying that way.

'David?' Cathy Neave arrived at their table and frowned. 'Oh. I didn't realise it wasn't just the two of us for lunch.'

'You remember Laura and Holly Jones, don't you, Mum?' David said.

'Um, yes.' Cathy gave Holly an embarrassed smile. 'How are you?'

Holly smiled back at her. 'Fine, thanks. Nice to see you again.'

Holly's father arrived next. 'Hello, love,' he said, kissing Holly's cheek. 'David. Cathy.' Harry nodded politely to both of them and took his place next to Laura.

'So what's this all about?' Laura asked.

Holly and David exchanged a glance. They'd both expected Laura to take charge and she hadn't disappointed them.

'It's about something that happened twelve years ago. When we were sitting our A levels,' Holly said.

'You've already told me, Mum, that you weren't completely honest with Holly about me going away, and you didn't pass on her messages,' David said. 'And you made sure I didn't get her letters.'

'And you didn't tell me David rang either,' Holly said to her mother.

Cathy and Laura both looked extremely uncomfortable. 'You were only eighteen. You were too young to know what you were doing,' Laura said.

'We thought it would be best if—' Cathy began.

'Hang on. Who's this ''we''?' David asked.

'Laura and Harry and me,' Cathy said.

'So *you* knew I was pregnant, too?' Holly frowned. 'But...' She shook her head in puzzlement. 'How?'

'I told her,' Laura said. 'In the circumstances, I thought she should know. And we both agreed it was too much for you to cope with. You had your whole lives ahead of you.'

'So you made sure we split up,' David said quietly. He slid his arm round Holly's shoulders. 'We found each other again in the end, and we're back together. But you took twelve years from us. Twelve years when we could have been happy.'

'You were little more than children at the time,' Cathy said. 'I was a single mum, and although I love you dearly and I've never regretted having you, even for a second, I know how hard it can be. I know many sacrifices you'd have had to make. You couldn't possibly have studied to become a doctor and brought up a baby at the same time. Neither of you could have done it.'

'When you have children of your own you'll understand,' Harry said. 'We thought we were acting for the best. Stopping you making a mistake you'd have regretted for the rest of your lives.'

David and Holly exchanged a glance. Hurdle one over. Now for the second.

'What if I told you I was pregnant now?' Holly asked. 'Pregnant and unmarried?'

Laura sighed. 'We'd be disappointed. Of course we would—wouldn't we, Harry? But I suppose you're old enough to make your own decisions.'

'And if I told you I'd got a girl into trouble, Mum?' David asked.

Cathy folded her arms. 'It depends how you feel about Holly. If you love her, marry her. If you don't love each other, you'll only make each other unhappy, so you'd have to think very hard about what you're going to do. But I'd expect you to provide for the child and be a proper father, at the very least.'

'Are you telling us—?' Laura began.

'We're going to have a baby,' David cut in. 'Hol and I. You're going to be grandparents.'

There was a long, long silence. Then Harry asked, 'Are you planning to get married?'

'What if we're not?' Holly asked.

'Well, of course you—' Laura began.

'That's your decision,' Harry said, overriding her.

'Agreed,' Cathy said.

Laura said nothing but looked miserable.

Holly took pity on her mother. 'Yes, we are going to get married.'

'It's taken us long enough,' David added.

Hurdle three. 'But I am definitely *not* wearing a meringue dress,' Holly said. 'And we're not getting married in church.'

'It's your day, so it's your decision,' Cathy said. 'But if there's anything I can do to help, any running around you want done, just tell me.'

Holly smiled at her in relief. 'So you don't mind? I always felt you thought I was…well, too posh for David.'

Cathy shrugged. 'If you love each other, that's all that matters.' She kissed Holly's cheek. 'Welcome to the family, love.'

'Oh, I love him all right,' Holly said softly. 'I've loved him for nearly half my life.'

David raised her hand to his lips. 'That goes for me, too.' He looked at Laura. 'I don't believe in class barriers. I am who I am.'

Laura squirmed. 'I, um…'

'Welcome to the family, son.' Harry reached over to shake David's hand. 'I know you both invited us here, but I insist that lunch is going to be on me, as the father of the bride-to-be. Our family celebration. And we're having champagne.' He beckoned the waiter over and ordered a bottle.

'Not for me, thanks. I can't face it, not even a sip,' Holly admitted when the waiter was filling their glasses.

Cathy squeezed her hand. 'When you get to fourteen weeks you'll feel a lot better.' She smiled. 'I was the same with David. The end result's worth it.'

'It had better be,' Holly said wryly. 'I'm sick of living on cornflakes and dry toast.'

Laura had been silent for so long that Holly stared at her mother. 'Mum? Are you all right?'

Laura dabbed at her eyes with a tissue. 'You're getting married. And I'm going to be a grandmother. I…I don't know what to say.' She sniffed. 'Except... When you do have the scan, please can I have a copy of the photograph?'

'The major one's in seven weeks' time,' David said. 'But we do have a picture from an earlier scan.'

Holly fished it from her bag and passed it to her mother, who stared at it as if it was the most precious thing in the world, then handed it reverently to Cathy.

'Our grandchild. It's incredible—we didn't have these in my day,' Cathy said. 'Everything was all right, wasn't it?'

Holly nodded. 'We had a slight scare a couple of weeks ago. That's why we waited until now before telling you— David insisted that I rested. For *days*.'

'And you obeyed him?' Harry chuckled. 'I wish I'd seen that.'

'I had to resort to blackmail,' David said with a grin.

Oh, no. Surely he wasn't going to tell them?

To her relief, he didn't. He just grinned again. 'Except I think the threat I used might not work any more.'

He was right there, she thought, and kicked his ankle under the table.

'So where are you getting married?' Cathy asked.

'We wanted somewhere different. We did think about London Zoo, but it'll be too cold really. So we're getting married where I proposed,' David said. 'A historic building.'

Laura looked slightly mollified. 'A stately home?'

'Not *exactly*,' Holly said. 'Tower Bridge.'

'But—' Laura began.

'That's unusual,' Harry said.

At the same moment Cathy said, 'Amazing!'

'So you won't want my WI group doing your flowers,' Laura said.

Holly saw the hint of a tear glittering in her mother's eyes and felt guilty. She reached for David's hand and squeezed it. 'We'd be delighted to have them do the christening flowers—wouldn't we, David?'

'Next summer,' David said.

'We'll organise it. The parish church looks really—' Laura began.

'Mum, the christening's going to be in London. Where we live,' Holly said gently. 'Where our baby's going to be brought up.'

'Of course.' Laura sat ramrod-straight, a sign Holly knew of old. It meant that her mother was disappointed and putting on a brave face. 'Have you decided on a date for the wedding?'

'Next month,' Holly said. 'It's midweek, but that means more of our friends can make it.'

'But there's so much to do! You can't organise a wedding that quickly. Not properly,' Laura said.

David spread his hands. 'I think you're underestimating your daughter, Mrs Jones.'

'Laura,' she corrected him wryly.

'What's there to organise?' Holly asked. 'The invitations are being printed and we're sending them out with Christmas cards; the caterer, florist and photographer are booked; the cake's ordered—oh, and by the way, it's chocolate, because David *hates* fruit cake; Jude and Zo have already dragged me to find dresses for all three of us; David's hiring morning dress; and we're leaving for our hotel by boat, which is also booked.' She shrugged. 'It's all done.'

'Definitely a chip off the old block,' Harry said, laughing. 'I don't think even your mother could sort things that quickly.'

'So there's nothing we can do?' Cathy said.

'Just be there and enjoy yourselves,' David said. 'And be happy for us.'

Cathy lifted her glass. 'Then I propose a toast. To Holly, David, our new family.'

'Holly, David, our new family and our first grandchild,' Harry and Laura echoed.

'And the beginning of a lifetime of happiness,' David added.

MILLS & BOON®

Live the emotion

Medical
romance™

THE DOCTOR'S RESCUE MISSION *by Marion Lennox*

(Air Rescue)

A tidal wave has swept across Petrel Island. Houses are destroyed, people are injured. In the wake of this disaster the Air-Sea Rescue team – led by Dr Grady Reece – flies in to help. Grady finds dedicated doctor Morag Lacy in charge. Morag and Grady once had a blazing affair and a brilliant future – but she left him to be the island doctor. Is this Grady's chance to win her back?

THE LATIN SURGEON *by Laura MacDonald*

(Mediterranean Doctors)

Nurse Lara Gregory gets off to a bad start with locum consultant Andres Ricardo. Wealthy and darkly handsome, he seems as out of place at her burns unit as she would in his lavish London lifestyle. But Andres is the most caring surgeon Lara has ever worked with, and soon she's thinking about him far too much!

DR CUSACK'S SECRET SON *by Lucy Clark*

Dr Rachael Cusack never expected to see her one and only true love again. He broke her heart and unknowingly left her pregnant. Now she has a wonderful son and an independent life – the gorgeous Joe Silvermark is the last thing on her mind. Then, on her first day in a new practice, she finds herself face to face with the father of her child…

On sale 1st April 2005

Available at most branches of WHSmith, Tesco, ASDA, Martins, Borders, Eason, Sainsbury's and all good paperback bookshops.

Visit www.millsandboon.co.uk

New York Times Bestselling Author

Vicki Lewis Thompson
Stephanie Bond
Judith Arnold

Three brand-new novellas!

Fool For Love

Available from 1st April 2005

Available at most branches of WHSmith,
Tesco, ASDA, Martins, Borders, Eason, Sainsbury's
and most good paperback bookshops.

FREE!
4 Books
and a surprise gift!

We would like to take this opportunity to thank you for reading this Mills & Boon® book by offering you the chance to take FOUR more specially selected titles from the Medical Romance™ series absolutely FREE! We're also making this offer to introduce you to the benefits of the Reader Service™—

- ★ FREE home delivery
- ★ FREE gifts and competitions
- ★ FREE monthly Newsletter
- ★ Exclusive Reader Service offers
- ★ Books available before they're in the shops

Accepting these FREE books and gift places you under no obligation to buy, you may cancel at any time, even after receiving your free shipment. Simply complete your details below and return the entire page to the address below. You don't even need a stamp!

YES! Please send me 4 free Medical Romance books and a surprise gift. I understand that unless you hear from me, I will receive 6 superb new titles every month for just £2.75 each, postage and packing free. I am under no obligation to purchase any books and may cancel my subscription at any time. The free books and gift will be mine to keep in any case.

M5ZEF

Ms/Mrs/Miss/Mr ....Initials ....

Surname .... BLOCK CAPITALS PLEASE

Address ....

....

....Postcode ....

Send this whole page to:
UK: FREEPOST CN81, Croydon, CR9 3WZ